TREEHOUSE Summer

C.S. ROCKROHR

Copyright © 2022 C.S. Rockrohr.

All rights reserved. No part of this book may be reproduced, stored, or transmitted by any means—whether auditory, graphic, mechanical, or electronic—without written permission of both publisher and author, except in the case of brief excerpts used in critical articles and reviews. Unauthorized reproduction of any part of this work is illegal and is punishable by law.

ISBN: 979-8-88640-391-6 (sc)
ISBN: 979-8-88640-392-3 (hc)
ISBN: 979-8-88640-393-0 (e)

Because of the dynamic nature of the Internet, any web addresses or links contained in this book may have changed since publication and may no longer be valid. The views expressed in this work are solely those of the author and do not necessarily reflect the views of the publisher, and the publisher hereby disclaims any responsibility for them.

One Galleria Blvd., Suite 1900, Metairie, LA 70001
1-888-421-2397

CHAPTER 1

School's Out

The way Skip Chapman had it figured, there sure was a lot time wasted bringing kids back for only three hours on the last day of school. Oh sure, he thought as he fidgeted at his desk, the party is nice and it's important to tell friends goodbye, but by June 1st summer's almost here, and there are so many great things to do!

Skip looked down for the hundredth time at the tattered tablet on top of his belongings. His mind wandered to his summer project as he studied the treehouse plans he had opened in front of him. The plans had been done over a year ago, and the work was already started; so he was thinking of the next few steps he would have to take and thinking about the building materials he needed to gather.

His attention was brought back to the fifth grade classroom when Mrs. Hanson announced that the class should take one last look around their room before leaving it for good. She spoke to each pupil at the door and read their names as she handed out report cards, wishing them well in middle school. In spite of the excitement of summer break, no one pushed or talked while Mrs. Hanson bade her pupils goodbye. It was a special moment and they sensed it. They spilled out slowly and resumed chatting with their friends as they walked to the cafeteria for the last time.

Skip and several of his closest friends sat around a table (nearest the pizza, cupcakes, and pop) and joked about how they were going to sleep until noon and then stay up all night playing video games and watching TV. Mike and Jerry talked about a campout they were planning at the dunes while Hatch whined about having to go to summer school again. Skip told the guys more about the plans he had for his treehouse. "It's gonna be great, it's gonna have real windows and best of all, it's gonna be totally private." Skip shook his head and vowed, "Probably no one'll bother me anyway 'cause it's clear out past the orchard – 'specially no little sister," he grinned.

"Yeah," Mike agreed, "That's how it should be. When my dad helped me build mine he never told me I would have to share it with my goofy little brothers...'cause if he woulda told me that," he paused and grunted, "I woulda said forget it!" he emphasized, thumping his chest with his fingers.

The student body was bathed in bright sunshine and scorching June heat when the students began exiting the school building. Skip high-fived his friends and waved to others as he scanned the waiting buses and cars. He spotted the family van and ran to it, slid the door open, hopped in and tossed his backpack over the seat in what appeared to his Mother as one fluid motion.

"Hi Mom! Seen Pen yet?" She turned to greet him, "Hi yourself...how about closing that door because I haven't seen anyone from her class yet, so it may be a few minutes. Meanwhile we can't be air conditioning the whole outdoors."

Skip slid over and shut the door. "Dang it I wanted to get away fast, you know beat the traffic and stuff. Hope we get to the farm way before dark."

Well it really wasn't a farm. Used to be with cows, chickens and fields of feed corn, when it belonged to Uncle Lawrence. Skip's mother, Shirley Chapman, was Lawrence's niece and she inherited, it at his passing. At the time, it didn't seem like much because Uncle Lawrence had kept everything he had ever owned and eventually ended up living in two rooms and a bath as the other rooms filled with junk. He also never cleaned much; so the family had a huge task on their hands that whole first summer, hoeing out, scrubbing and finally redecorating the aging farmhouse. Last summer was better, though, because the place was easily cleaned and settled, and the majority of the acreage was leased out; so it felt more like their home. Then, there was the bonus of the giant gnarled tree behind the orchard that Skip discovered. All winter long, he sketched and planned, checking with his Dad as necessary. They had worked on the framing together just before returning to Lincoln last fall. Jim Chapman wanted his son to have the experience he had when he was a boy; building a treehouse, but also needed to be sure it was going to be safe. Jim's memories of his own treehouse gave him the jitters. Especially the bracing. He recalled his Dad making him tear it three quarters of the way down and then they rebuilt it together. It was a good memory though; all the time spent with his father. He was as eager as Skip to start it last summer. He told Skip lots of stories along the way and they had plenty of fun.

Just about everyday someone in the family mentioned something they wanted to do "out at the farm." Everyone worked feverishly beginning early in May in anticipation of the move and eagerly made the trip last weekend to take clothes, groceries and the pets down.

"There's Penny," Shirley announced and Skip quickly slid over and opened the van door letting in Penny and her humongous backpack.

He pulled it off her as she exclaimed "Mommie guess what? I got permoted! Know what else? I got Mr. Caskin for second grade and not mean ole Mrs. Willet…she's sooooo mean 'cause on raining days she just makes you work, work, work, but Mr.

Caskin lets the class play games." She sucked in half a breath. "I'm really gla..."

"Penny!" her mother interrupted "Please slow down Honey, we'll all have plenty of time to talk on the trip down." She said gently to her excited daughter.

Skip flopped back on his seat. "Yeah nobody can say anything when you're yakking because you don't even take a breath. You need to breathe for a while, Penny; your lungs are probably ready to collapse." Skip added. Penny pretty much missed out on his speech though because she was waving frantically at friends as the van pulled past a loaded school bus.

"Well Skip, then how about you? Did you get promoted?" his mother inquired as she peeked at him in the rear view mirror.

"Course I did!" He sat upright. "Report card's pretty good, really," he allowed "but I got a C in current events on account of my globe. 'Member that project I did?"

"Mmmm." She mused "Sure do that was quite the weekend."

"Well most of my labels fell off" he admitted "and I couldn't remember where very many were supposed to be, so Mrs. Hanson went and marked it down because she didn't think I was prepared."

"Hey I got a mark too! For additube." Penny announced.

Shirley's eyebrows shot up and Skip quickly looked at the seven year old's progress report.

"That's *at-ti-tuduh, silly*, and it means you have a *good* attitude... kinda how you are in class, like trying hard and being cheerful about your work."

Shirley smiled. "Good job clearing that up, Skip. I was about to stop the car and find out why a first grader would get marked down in deportment."

Penny's eyes got saucer like as she slid down into the seat, not really sure what was going on but relieved that her mother hadn't stopped the car and also wondering what in the world deportment was. She mumbled to herself, "I'm a *second* grader," thinking that her Mother had already forgotten.

The kids leaned forward as Shirley stopped at the curb in front of Jim Chapman's office building.

"Will Daddy be ready to go Mommie? I can't hardly wait no more." "Oh Penny, such grammar."

"Guess he will, "announced Skip." There he is now, just coming out."

Penny grabbed her report off her lap and climbed out of the van to walk to the corner with her father and help him mail the stack of envelopes he carried.

Skip sat staring at the nameplate on the side of the brick building that read; C. James Chapman and Associates. "Mrs. Hanson called me Carlton James Chapman the third, today when she gave me my report card Mom, and some of the kids laughed." He paused. "I don't get it, "Gramps is Carlton James Chapman, and people call him Carl. Dad is Carlton James Chapman the second and everyone calls him Jim. I'm Carlton James Chapman the third, and you all call me Skip." He held up his hands in exasperation... "Couldn't we just have been named what you call us anyhow?"

Shirley laughed. "Would we call Gramps Carl or Gramps?" Skip shook his head, "You know what I mean Mom," he replied, making a face, "real names, just not so fancy."

Shirley watched her husband and daughter as they approached. "I certainly do Carlton, after all that really *is* your name."

Skip leaned over the seat to read his Mothers laughing eyes. "On second thought why not forget this conversation even took place and just leave things the way they are" he grinned sheepishly. "I guess I'd prefer Skip for a while yet, say maybe until I leave for college. Okay?" he said briskly, signaling his Mom to drop it.

The door slid open and Penny jumped in. Jim stretched into the backseat to assist Penny with her seatbelt. As he opened his door and climbed into the seat beside Shirley, Penny shrieked, "Mommie! Guess what?" not waiting for an answer; actually, no one ever really attempted to answer Penny's rapidly fired "guess whats?" "Daddy says we can go to Mr. Beefy! And guess what? I get the corner seat! He said so," she shouted as she shot an, "and that's final, "kind of look at Skip. "Right Daddy?"

"Whoa there, hang on a minute" her father protested as he reached toward her, holding up a finger to signal *no more talking*. "That was a month ago when we went to the mall. Yes," he explained, "I said we're going to Mr. Beefy but I'm talking about the one by the interstate and I don't recall if it even has a corner seat...who knows, maybe it's round inside."

"Skip snickered quietly "Yeah, like the big hole in your head." Penny's mouth dropped and her eyes bugged as she gasped, preparing to tell on him.

"Just kidding Pen," he added hastily, looking to see if his parents had picked up his taunt. Fortunately they were greeting each other with a kiss and he whistled quietly, in relief, well aware of how quickly he could go *too* far with his teasing, especially on a long drive in the car.

By the time the Chapman van rolled into the farmyard, Penny and Skip had settled down after talking at length about the last day at school. Suddenly Penny broke the silence. "Higby and Snuff! Are we going to Gramma's to get them tonight Daddy?"

Higby was their toy collie and Snuff their cat, so named when she was the fifth kitten being born one afternoon at Aunt Betty's when Penny exclaimed" that's s'nough." So the name stuck and now Snuff was a full-grown tabby and an important member of the Chapman family.

Jim stretched his arms and spoke through a yawn. "Oh I doubt that they are even home Penny, they usually go into Barlow on Friday night. We'll go for Higby and Snuff right away in the morning. After all, we just brought them down last week. They haven't forgotten us yet."

Just about the time Penny was going to start to pout, the side door in the barn opened. Higby burst out and rushed to greet everyone as they climbed out of the van on stiffened legs. Gramps wasn't far behind him.

"Hi gang!" he called out over the barking. "Glad you're finally here. Gramma made strawberry shortcake but wouldn't give me any 'til you got here." Skip would have been the first one in the farmhouse but his dad managed three steps to his one. Then Higby ran between his legs on a tear and got through the door second, sliding partway down the hallway, missing the kitchen altogether. After much chatter and strawberry shortcake, the grandparents left to walk the quarter mile down the dirt road to their lake cottage, and Skip and Penny who had been pushing their luck since arriving, were sent off to bed. Skip was tired, to be sure, but he still had enough energy to go over his plans and unpack his wooden sign for the front of the tree house. If Penny had any thoughts at all, they came in the form of dreams because she fell asleep as soon as she got her stuffed animals situated around her. After all she was "permoted" today. That can take a lot out of a barely-seven year old girl.

"Ahh!" sighed the weary accountant as he eased himself into the chaise lounge on the front porch of the old farmhouse. "Just think Shirley. Three whole weeks off. No traffic jams, no pollution, no hysterical clients. I don't think that I have ever been as ready for a vacation as I am right now." His arm dropped accidentally onto Higby who took it for a signal to play and bounded off the steps in search of his ball.

"Well you certainly have earned your vacation Jim. What are you going to do first?

"Well!" he announced thoughtfully, "Tomorrow afternoon I'm going to begin to restore that chiffierobe I bought at the auction last summer, since I have everything I need for it right here. It's a beauty Shirl...in great condition inside and out. I pulled out the shelves and took off the hardware last weekend. You know, I decided this past week during one of my mental trips out to the farm," he laughed "that I'd like to enter it in the fair in August. That's why I need to get started."

Sounds like it didn't take long to shake those office blues Jim; I know you've been under a lot of pressure."

He nodded "You can say that again, but I promise you this, I will not talk shop at all, these next three weeks. Count on it."

Shirley stood up and yawned. "Well you're the accountant so you're in charge of counting, but I'm sure about something too." Stretching, she continued, "I can't wait to crawl into that big old bed. Your mom opened up the windows and it's nice and cool up there." She leaned and kissed him on top of his head.

He waved her off. "Sure, go ahead. I'll be up shortly. Just need to check Higby's water and get down my tackle box. Dad and I are going fishing early tomorrow morning." He turned toward the empty doorway and thought, "I'm talking to a screen door. Didn't get away from that office a minute too soon."

CHAPTER II

Crash!!!

By nine in the morning the whole family was up and busy. The men were out fishing on the lake long before anyone else was up. Shirley and grandmother Wilma were working on the tangled grapevines beside the tool shed. Penny was scurrying all around the yard looking for all the new kittens the two barn cats had produced over the winter. Snuff was exploring with Penny, and began jumping up old hay bales in the barn after a young bird that was flitting and floundering in the rafters. Penny was right behind the cat that was in pursuit of the bird.

Skip was beginning to tire from numerous trips to the barn and through the orchard to his tree house site. "Just a few more pieces and I'll be all set," he thought. As he approached the barn for another load of wood, he heard a loud crash. That was followed by a scream and then a yowl. He dropped the handle to the wagon and hurried through the gaping barn door to investigate. He was surprised by Snuff who came flying out, feet scarcely touching the ground.

Once inside Skip saw the problem immediately. Penny was sitting on a tangled pile of boards in a huge sunlit dust cloud. "I almost caught that bird," she sobbed. "But that darn old workbench broke and dumped me and I hurt my el-booowssssss" she oohed and hissed in pain.

"See Skip." She held up her arm for Skip to examine.

"Wow!" he exclaimed, "Will you look at that!"

Penny's tear filled eyes shot a frightened look at Skip as she wriggled her arm around trying to get a glimpse of her injury. "Is it *that* bad Skip?" She cried in panic as she tumbled off the wood and struggled to her feet, "Mommie!" She shrieked, running past Skip.

Skip stammered, "N...No Penny... it's just that I... this... Penny wait!" he called to no avail. Skip stood spellbound at his good fortune as he stared down at the stack of scrap wood. "Aww-right! This is exactly what I need!" He bent down to sort the boards. "Three, four, five, six, seven! This'll take care of the whole floor." "Boy," he thought, "Penny really did me a favor, bustin down that old workbench 'cause I would have never found this great wood." Feeling new energy, he busied himself carrying the boards to the tree house all the while expecting his mother to show up at the "scene of the accident" which he was sure Penny had greatly exaggerated.

The rest of the morning Skip cheerfully finished hauling the wood and was nailing down the last plank of the floor when Penny came running through the orchard calling, "Skiiiiip! Luuunch-tiiime!" He looked down and watched his sister scampering his way, gesturing and hollering the whole time.

She arrived winded. "Oh Skip! It's so big! Can I come up?" Skip scrambled towards the ladder. "Not yet, I've got junk all over up here. Like it, huh?" he asked as he descended.

Penny beamed, "its bee-yoo-tee-ful"

He stepped over some scraps to where she stood. "Well I didn't really plan to make it beautiful...but guess you just don't know many treehouse words yet, huh?" Skip smiled as he swatted at Penny's ponytails and asked about her elbow the same way any big brother would do when he's feeling great, and

Skip really was feeling great as he glance back over his shoulder at his carpentry. "I'm going to sleep out here sometimes, maybe Dad too." he blurted.

Penny turned her big brown eyes up to him and opened her mouth to speak but Skip cut her off.

"Forget it." he said with certainty. As her head dropped along with her lower lip, he asked quickly, "So, wanna race? I'll give you a head start!" At that, she was off as fast as her slightly little legs could carry her, screeching the entire distance to the house.

CHAPTER III

The Chiffierobe

Once inside the cool kitchen, Skip realized how tired he really was as he plopped down heavily on the bench under the big kitchen window.

"My word Skipper, it is only noon. You look bushed," remarked his grandfather.

"I am Gramps, from hauling wood all morning, but I'll be ready to go again after lunch" he replied as his arms dropped dead weight between his outstretched legs. "I hope so anyway "he sighed to the floor. "You guys catch anything?"

"Mud turtle. Going to have mud turtle soup for lunch. Same color as mud!"

Skip looked at Penny, knowing his Grampa was teasing, as usual. "Ewwwww! Do I hafta eat it, Mommie?" They all laughed and Penny relaxed.

"Hey let's eat before I get too comfortable, here, my legs are starving I think." Skip urged.

"Say! That's right" recalled his father, "The tree house. How is it going son? Being careful with that saw, I hope. We don't need another catastrophe," nodding toward Penny who held up her arm, brightly decorated with a smiley face bandage, "especially on our first day of vacation."

"Sure I'm being careful but luckily I'm not going to have to cut a whole lot more anyhow. The boards I found on the scrap pile are fine just the way they are. In fact, I just nailed the last one down when Penny called me for lunch."

Skip peeled himself off the bench and went to the sink to wash up. "Boy Dad, Uncle Lawrence sure had a lot of neat stuff."

"You've heard the saying Skip, "Some peoples trash is someone else's treasure." Said his mother as she placed a plate of sloppy joes on the table.

Skip nodded. "Well, all I know is it's lucky for me because my tree house is going to be terrific."

Penny popped up, "And beautiful."

He looked gratefully at his little sister. "Sorry you got hurt though Penny."

Penny enjoyed the attention and took time to be sure everyone was getting another look at her arm.

"Speaking of beautiful Dad," Jim said between bites," you should come out to the tool shed with me after lunch and see my blue ribbon chiffierobe."

Carl raised his eyebrows. "Blue ribbon, no less?" nodding to the family to emphasize Jim's remark.

"Yes Sir," replied Jim," I'm planning to enter it in the fair. It might be my best restoration project yet. I'm anxious to see it's original color" he grinned. I think it's going to be a big job though because I'd venture a guess that it's eight feet tall and nearly that wide too. I know it was a job for Frank and I to move it from the barn to the workshop last week."

Wilma passed a bowl of chips to her husband and said"Sounds a lot like the one Sally and Pete have, doesn't it Carl?"

Gramps cocked his head and stared at the bowl he held, "You know" he nodded, "it does, now that you mention it." He laughed. "I guarantee you though theirs can't possibly be in useful condition anymore if he left it out all the last two years." He searched his memory. "Yes I'm sure last I saw it was when they auctioned his herd out at their farm, it was out on the back porch. One door was missing and some of the hardware had been taken off...probably to use on something else." He thought back, "But I remember when it was in good shape. Beautiful piece. Limited edition from the old Andersonville cabinet factory, I'm sure. Pete has funny ideas about what's valuable just like Lawrence did." He concluded.

"My mother told me years ago "Wilma recalled," that my oldest brothers would both be collectors or junk men. She was right. They both were both! They just never knew it."

Shirley and Jim shook their heads in agreement Jim said, "Well maybe my project is only of value to me anyway, who knows? I'm ready to go on it though. I've decided not to sell this piece. We can use it in the den."

"We really can Jim, this place has already started to take on that cluttered look it had when Uncle Lawrence lived here," lamented Shirley

"Oh puleeze not that again!" protested Penny. The whole group marveled at her reaction when Shirley tried to recall how it would have seemed like work to Penny, who played between every little "chore" she was given all the time the rest of the family worked on the farmhouse.

Carl stretched as they rose from the table, and reached for his hat and said "Jim, I'll stop back over later, I want to sneak home and catch forty winks."

Penny perked up from playing with her sandwich. "Oooh Gramps can I go? I never saw four-d-wings."

The Chapman grandparents looked at Penny's smiling parents and when Shirley nodded, Gramps said, "Sure, I could use the help because I usually fall asleep waiting for them to come."

Penny jumped off her chair and grabbed her grandfather's hand "Don't you worry Gramps, I can stay awake for a day and a night and two tomorrows." She turned back at the door, "I'll be home later Mommie, 'case you need me."

CHAPTER IV

The Dragonfly

Later in the week, Penny sat on the side of her grandparents dock and dangled her bare feet in the cool water. Occasionally a tiny fish would nibble at her toes and she would concentrate real hard at not moving and scaring the fish away. Big blue dragonflies landed briefly on the dock and on the boat that was tied up to a stake on the shoreline. The dragonfly that fascinated her, though, was one that had landed on the tippy-top of a water reed near the shore and stayed there. It was so close to Penny that she could see the lacy features of its wings.

"Penny! Don't get too far out on that dock," called Gramma from the patio up the hill. Penny didn't want to answer her grandmother because she didn't want to frighten away the fish or the dragonflies. But she realized that if she didn't acknowledge her grandmother, Gramma would come all the way down to the lake to remind her, as always, that even though she can stand up in the water at the end of the dock, she was required to have an adult or Skip there when she's in the water.

"Okay, I won't," she called up. The fish all scattered with her slight movement, but the dragonfly stayed on the top of the reed. "Maybe he can't hear me she thought. I wish I could touch him and let him sit on my finger."

"Dragonfly," she sang. "Here dragonfly...come to Penny." The dragonfly didn't come but it wasn't frightened by the outstretched arm either. Penny looked around and spotted a stick on the ground in front of the boat.

"Maybe you don't feel good dragonfly," she said, "All your friends are flying around." She got up quietly and the motion sent the little fish scurrying for the shadow of the dock. "Bye l'il fishies, see you later," she whispered as she tiptoed softly off the dock and walked over to the patch of grass to get the stick she planned to use to reach the dragonfly. Once she picked up the stick, though, she started wondering if the stick would scare the dragonfly. It was then that she realized that the back of her grandpa's boat was very near the dragonfly. Slowly she crept to the boat and stepped one foot into it causing it to creak loudly, and prompting her to freeze half-in and half-out. The dragonfly still didn't move. As she gingerly climbed into the boat she said, "Now I get it, you're sleeping. You don't even know I'm here." Penny took two more steps and straddled the middle seat. The boat shifted and rocked.

"Penny" called her grandmother from the bedroom window, "don't untie the boat. Daddy and Grampa didn't pull it far enough onto the shore." Penny looked at the stake and nodded an exaggerated nod as she put a finger to her mouth to show Gramma to be quiet.

Wilma smiled, knowing full well that Penny had spotted a fish or something on the shallow shoreline and was intending to catch it for a pet, like she has been trying to do since she was four.

"Okay Honey," Gramma acknowledged. "You be sure to come in before it starts raining." Penny nodded again glancing absently at the sky. The dragonfly was still there even though Penny's ponytails were flopping around and the boat was creaking.

Penny coached herself as she talked softly to the dragonfly. "If I can just get you to walk onto my finger, I bet I could take you to my house." Slowly she tried to distract the pretty dragonfly by making idle chatter and said, "Do you know where I live? Did you ever fly by the farm house on Lake Road?" She crouched lower and stretched her neck. "It's right that way," she said enthusiastically and gestured by pointing. "Ooh... don't fly away, it's okay," she cooed. Penny leaned forward again pursing her lips in determination.

The wind picked up and caused the reeds to whistle and move as the boat pivoted and bumped into the patch. Then, just as quickly, the wind shifted and moved the rear of the boat several inches out of reach of the dragonfly. "Darn old wind, put me back," she said impatiently.

Penny heard the screen door shut at the cottage and turned to see her grandmother making her way down toward the shed on the other side of the dock. She turned back to discover that she had floated back toward the dragonfly even closer than before and held out her finger within a couple of inches of her goal. She had to pull her hand back though when Gramma startled her by banging the shed door shut and locking it.

Wilma Chapman turned toward Penny, calling over the rustling sound of blowing leaves, "Come along Penny, let's get inside before it..." Her voice blew away when a violent wind came noisily down the hillside blowing biting sand into her eyes. The boat lurched and Penny nearly fell down. She grabbed the side of the rocking boat to keep her balance. Rain began falling down in cold sheets chilling her quickly. Instantly darkness descended across the lakefront. Penny squinted, unable to open her eyes, in the rain and wind. Thunder shook her surroundings and vibrated the boat. Suddenly, a bolt of lightning hit nearby, lighting up the shoreline. Penny opened her eyes by shielding them and screamed when she heard a deafening crack. She covered her face as a large limb slammed onto the bank, and into the water. The longest branches reached toward her, hitting the front of her grandparent's boat. The impact caused the whole boat to shudder and knocked Penny off her seat when she let go in order to cover her head.

The boat already had accumulated water in all the grooves on the floor and it was slippery. Penny rolled off her stinging bottom and climbed onto her knees, steadying herself with her forearms on the seat she had been unceremoniously knocked from. Branches were reaching out all over her grandparent's lot and half of the large trunk stretched part way up the hill. Penny could make out the bright blond wood from the portion of the tree still standing and could smell sour smoke. She positioned herself to peek through the leafy barricade and searched the shore for her grandmother. She was going to need help to get past the branches and on to the shore in the darkness. She blinked her eyes and stared at the unusual sights along the shoreline. Another bolt of lightning struck nearby. Penny was terrified by the eerie light as she became aware of her position. She shook violently and confirmed with a second flash what the light had revealed. She screamed in horror.

One of the long limbs had hit the shed, crushing the roof and collapsing the front. Penny strained to see through the leafy mound and spotted where her grandmother was trapped under its branches and leaves. Penny could best see a yellow sweater sleeve. "Gramma! Gramma! Get up! She cried, "We have to go inside!" The thunder was constant. She knew she was not being heard. Penny moved closer to the front of the boat and began tugging at the branches that held her at bay. The small branch she was tugging on broke, causing her to lose her balance again and fall backward, plopping down hard on the floor of the boat. The sudden shift in weight did the trick though because the boat slid out from under the bushy branches.

"Good! I'm coming, Gramma," she cried as she tried to regain her footing to step out and wade in, but she was hampered by the rocking of the boat. It was then that she caught a glimpse of the rope with a broken piece of stake tied to it, slip into the water.

She screamed again at the now bloody yellow arm waving and thrashing. "Gramma! Help me! Please get up!"

It began raining very hard again and the wind blew with tremendous force, pushing the little rowboat swiftly from the shore. Penny screamed a long high pitched scream that hurt her throat. Outdone by the thunder and lightning as well as the hard rain hitting the water, Penny surrendered and laid her head down on her knees and covered it with her arms. She began sobbing as the boat stole out onto the stormy lake. In a panicked voice heard only by her, she blubbered "Oh please…please somebody help us!"

CHAPTER V

Lost

Skip was grumbling as he gathered tools and watched his treehouse sketches rip free from the tacks on the plywood wall and blow away in the sudden storm. He scrambled to the ladder but couldn't get on it with so many tools in his hands. He tossed them ahead and hurried down missing two rungs in his haste. The icy rain was hurting his face and arms as he scrambled to gather the tools. He ran toward the dim silhouette of the barn dodging small branches that had already come down from the apple trees, young green apples still attached. He snagged his foot in some high grass when he veered from the familiar path in the darkness. Pulling free he kept his eyes on the barn and picked up his pace. As he rounded the corner of the barn, Skip saw his dad tugging at the swaying barn door. "Want some help?" he yelled over the roar of the wind coming between the buildings.

"No, I can get it, "Jim called out. "Hurry in and help your mother with the windows!"

Skip ran for the house and saw several baskets blow off the porch, rolling away like tumbleweed. He felt goose bumps run up his arms when the baskets disappeared in the midday storm. As he reached for the screen door he heard his mother banging around upstairs. He dropped his tools on the rag rug by the door.

Shivering, he felt a cold breeze coming from the den and hurried to close the windows. The den door blew shut nearly slamming him in the face. He pushed it open forcefully and rushed to close the two big windows.

Shirley was relieved to see Skip when she got back down to the kitchen and grateful to see that he had closed the den windows. "Well, I almost made it," she gasped. "Your dresser and headboard are all wet."

Skip sat down to take off his wet shoes. "Well, I almost didn't make it. That door slammed shut and missed my nose by this much." He measured out an inch with his fingers.

The kitchen door flew open and Jim Chapman burst in thoroughly soaked. "Boy!" he exclaimed, this one came up fast! The wind kept lifting the bottom of the barn door and it wouldn't glide. Finally got it though." He looked around the kitchen as he sat down to remove his boots. "Where's Penny?"

"Oh, she's down at your mother's," Shirley responded as she handed him a towel. "Your dad went to Langtry's to get milk and eggs and said he'd bring her home when he brings us our milk and eggs. I suppose it wouldn't hurt to check on your Mom and Penny though. They were staying home so she could bake pies and Penny was going to catch fish." Shirley signed with her hands to emphasize 'catch fish.'

Skip chuckled as he drew himself a glass of water. "Penny fishing...now that's funny. Remember when we took her out last summer Dad? She didn't sit still, she didn't shut up and she didn't keep her line in the water for even two minutes!"

Jim turned from the window and joined his son at the sink. "I sure do and I remember that she was truly shocked that she didn't catch any fish, but ", he added, "you know I once knew a little boy down on the same lake, in the same boat several years ago who did the same thing!"

Skip made a face and grabbed the towel his dad had left in a heap on the counter. "I think he's making that up." He protested, talking to his mother. "I'm going to change my shirt and dry off my stuff."

Shirley was dialing the phone when she took the receiver away from her ear "Jim, listen to this."

Jim walked over and took the phone. "Trouble on the line somewhere. Forget it Shirl, you won't get through. They won't be able to fix the lines until this storm passes."

They both looked out the window. "Looks like it has pretty much blown over anyway. Dad and Penny will be here soon."

Carl could see that the electricity was out at the lake when he pulled into his driveway. He had seen tree damage all along the road and was focusing on his broken trellis as he pulled a milk jug and two dozen eggs out of the trunk.

The rain had let up some but the wind was still whistling through the pines and willow so Carl wasn't really sure if he had heard a voice or not until he recognized the voice of Charlie his neighbor as Charlie came running past him toward Carl's lakefront. "Carl! Come quick!" Carl hurriedly put the jug and cartons back in the trunk and slammed it shut.

He rushed to the slope and saw Charlie slipping and sliding down to the mass of broken branches and limbs. Charlie reached the site and began yelling to Wilma above the howl of the wind "Do you think you're hurt badly?" He placed his head close to the small opening in the foliage. "Okay….w…we'll get you out.

You need to try to calm down though." He coaxed her loudly. Carl reached him, breathless, and dropped to his knees. He clenched his teeth when he saw his wife lying there trapped and bleeding. Charlie leaned into Carl and shouted, "She was trying to tell me something Carl! Find out what it is while I go get my son and some tools."

Carl broke several branches away from Wilma's face and called to her. She was hysterical. "Try not to hurt yourself any worse, "he encouraged, as he assessed the complex situation. Her sweater arm was nearly shredded from her struggling and she was covered with deep scratches and blood. Her chin and forehead were already bruising.

The worried husband tried reaching in to her to comfort her but couldn't keep from falling over on the heap that held her down. Finally, the wind let up and he could hear her weakened voice, mid-sentence, "and if she's not in the house, she probably tried to go for help!"

Carl sat back on his feet in shock. "Penny!"

He leaned over to her again. "But you're hurt and freezing Wilma." She shot him a stern look. "Carl! I'm alright. Just get going!" she cried.

Carl met Charlie and his son on the bank and told them that he had to check the cottage for Penny but that he was pretty sure that she would have run home for help." Charlie's son twisted toward the lake.

"Mr. Chapman, I think she's in the boat." The three of them hurried around the bushy fallen limb in order to see the dock. "I saw her playing in it," he explained, "before the storm hit, but Mrs. Chapman was down there with her so I thought nothing of it 'til now." They all stopped cold and silent. Carl's face turned white and his body stiffened. "Its gone." he said in a voice that was barely audible, even in the calm.

CHAPTER VI

Adrift

Penny lifted the piece of smelly oilcloth from her head and looked out over the lake. She shivered from the cold and convulsed from crying. "Oh how can I get back to help my Gramma?" she fretted. She had already discovered that the oars were not in the boat but she decided that it didn't really matter when, for a few minutes, her mind had wandered to a time she had gone out in the boat with her dad and brother. She had begged to row, and on her first attempt she didn't get the oars in the water much at all, mostly because she couldn't quite sit down. When she pulled they came together too fast, and she fell backwards into her dad's arms. Skip, on the other hand, got wet. After a brief lesson, she tried again and, that time dug in deeper and tugged so hard that she almost pole-vaulted to Skip.

Penny giggled out loud, under the oilcloth, and then realized where she was, when she heard herself. She took a deep breath to help her remain calm and stuck her head out like a turtle. She began searching the lakeshore again. The water was rough now; constantly rocking the boat and making her lose her place. She was trying to look at the cottages along the shore to see where she might be, but they all looked alike. She looked for the bait shop and little store where she always got Juicy Fruit gum when she went with Gramps. Nothing was lit up, not even the orange and yellow sign that said BAIT. At one point she did spot the big docks and marina but wasn't sure where they were situated by land anyway. She could hear sirens in the distance and prayed that they were for her or her grandmother.

The memory of that scene, on the lakefront, caused her to again break into heavy sobs that took her breath away. She pulled the oilcloth back over her head and began to slip into a fitful slumber, waking off and on with a sudden shudder of the boat or because of her upset stomach and chills.

Stringy gray clouds, shredded by the storm, passed over the lake as thunder rumbled in the distance.

Penny jerked awake when the boat bumped something. She rubbed her cold feet, stood up stiffly and squinted in the bright daylight to see that she had drifted into a channel and hit a submerged log. She looked around the area. "This is the wrong shore!" she cried, angrily. Skip hunts for turtles and crawdads over here! I know where this is!" She could feel panic overwhelming her. "Nobody can see me here." She whimpered. Penny didn't like the channel because she had gone through it once before, at night with her father and Uncle Frank, when they went out fishing for bullheads. They caught several and that experience was enough for her. She never asked to go again and vowed she'd never look at another bullhead.

Penny studied the shore line in search of a way to get to it, thinking she could find her way home the way Skip did when he took her turtle hunting. There were fallen trees in the water, where the turtles sunned themselves and berry briars along high stony bluffs. Penny could see no place to wade in to dry land. The area was deserted, save for a couple of scary looking ancient lake cottages boarded up and overgrown with weeds.

"Still", she thought, "maybe I can get a hold of the log or something so I don't float back out." She started to look for a rope and remembered there was one already tied to the front of the boat. She worked her way to the side of the boat touching the log and then studied the rope hanging in the water off the front. Just as she was summoning courage to try to reach the rope, her eyes fell on the anchor. "Yes! I can put it in the water and then I'll wait for somebody to find me." She looked apprehensively at the sky, now tinged with thin pink lines, and stiffened at the thought of being alone on the lake overnight. Spurned on by that frightening prospect, Penny tugged the heavy cement-filled coffee can, eye-hooked to a slimy rope, onto the rim of the boat. She pushed with one hand while she balanced it with the other. The gritty can ground to the edge and plopped into the water, jerking the rope out of her hand and splashing her. The splash frightened her and she sat down whimpering weakly and blew on her dirty, smelly, and now stinging hand. She calmed when she spotted a turtle crawling across a log several feet inland. She wished she could follow him to shore. As she sat forlornly, wondering if she would ever be found and thinking about the dragonfly that surely blew away, Penny's ears picked up a sound other than that of the water lapping at the boat. There was a boat motor somewhere out there. She couldn't see anything but she could pick up the sound off and on. She called out, gruffly at first. "Help! I'm lost. Hel...llll...p. Can you hearrr me?" She listened, barely breathing to help her hear better. Nobody called back. Now she noticed noisy blue jays and a few peepers, signaling dusk was approaching. At least she could still hear the faint trolling motor. "It's getting closer!" she cried aloud. As she listened intently, she spotted a large boat out on the lake and recognized it as the county fireboat that her Uncle Frank showed her last summer. A man stood high on it with his hands to his face and moved his head and shoulders slowly back and forth. "I bet he's got bernokilars!" Then, as if anyone would dispute her, she whispered, "He's looking for me." She jumped up and began calling, waving wildly. "Hey! I'm over here!"

  She saw the man bend over and pick up something and was startled when a crackly voice said, "Sit down Penny, we're coming!" She dropped to the seat immediately and hugged herself with joy. Tears welled up in her eyes and she blinked them away. Again the big voice spoke. "She's just around the bend Frank, in the channel."

Now Penny could hear the little invisible boat speed up and saw it break through some nearby cattails. Penny's eyes again filled with hot tears when she saw her Grampa and Uncle Frank edging toward her in the weedy water. She picked up the hums of several other boats approaching but never took her eyes off of her smiling heroes as she choked back hysteria.

CHAPTER VII

Reunited

Betty Chapman was torn between sitting in the den with her injured mother-in-law or comforting Shirley her sister-in-law. Betty and Frank, who is Jim's older brother, live about a quarter mile further around the lake from their parents in the house that Jim and Frank grew up in. Frank is a member of the Barlow Volunteer Fire Department, so he heard the call concerning Penny come over the monitor. This was just minutes after he and Betty got the news, also over the monitor, that his mother had suffered minor injuries and that the paramedics were being dispatched to her. The couple quickly decided that they would go to the cottage and then he would go out with the search party.

An hour later Betty and her patched up mother-in-law were at Jim and Shirley's where there was electricity and everyone had agreed to meet. No one in the Barlow area had phone service. Wilma had a big goose egg on her head and bandages several places on both arms. She had been given a sedative and instructions to call her doctor if anything developed over night. Her only complaint was a headache and some dizziness, but she insisted those maladies were from being so upset and tense with worry about Penny.

Shirley stood motionless in the kitchen window. Skip sat on the window seat. Neither one said anything while they held vigil. Deep down Skip was angry that he hadn't been allowed to go help look for Penny. But his dad was so disturbed when they heard about Penny and then his grandmother was brought to the farm injured and crying, that he was afraid to push.

"Stay by your mother," Jim demanded as he rushed out to Frank's waiting truck. Skip could see his grandfather's car, already ahead of them on the road, and thought how hard it must be for him to leave and how impossible to stay.

Higby, having failed on several attempts at getting Skip's attention lay gloomily under the table and stared at the door. The house was uncommonly quiet. No one spoke for a long, long time.

Even though it was early evening the sun broke through the clouds and the birds announced that the storm indeed was over. "Shirley," beckoned Betty, "come sit down and have some coffee." Shirley turned and stared blankly at the big kitchen table set with steaming mugs of coffee and Gramma's strawberry and cherry pies. "I have to stay and watch" Shirley pleaded, turning back, her voice trembling.

"Then let me bring you something" Betty urged softly.

Shirley nodded slowly. "Just coffee then, "she agreed. I'll sit here on the bench." She turned to Skip who had not taken his eyes off the entrance to the driveway. Go have some pie and milk Skip, you haven't eaten for hours."

He turned and spoke softly to his mother. "Can I have it over here Mom?" he asked, his eyes filling with tears.

"Of course you can," she said softly as she turned back toward the window. Shirley gasped, "It's Frank's truck! They're back." Betty rushed to Shirley and held on to her shoulders as they watched. "They must know something Betty." Shirley turned and searched her sister in law's eyes ...her mind trailed and she turned away. Skip and Higby ran out the door.

"Betty?" cried a weakened voice from the doorway to the den. Both ladies rushed to help Wilma to a chair.

The screen door squeaked and Penny, clad in a bright yellow fireman jacket that went past her knees, ran in and over to the open arms of her grandmother. She was followed by her jubilant rescuers and equally relieved brother. Higby got right to sniffing the fishy feet and fingers of his playmate.

"Gramma! Oh you got hurt!" Penny cooed. "I tried to help you but the stake broke and I blowed away!" Her grandmother brushed Penny's snarled sticky bangs off her forehead. "I know honey, I heard you calling, and I couldn't help you either!" The two overjoyed storm victims agreed that everything was going to be alright now though and decided it was time to celebrate.

Shirley whisked Penny off briefly to get her bathed and in pajamas. When they returned, the families enjoyed a quick supper with a party atmosphere while they pieced together the unfolding of events. Penny had her audience transfixed at her account of the anchor and of the man "who knew my name," with the "bernokilars and crackle voice." What she didn't tell them was much at all about what she felt or how she managed out on the stormy lake for nearly two hours, so no one really knew what she had been through.

Within minutes of dropping her fork on her half eaten piece of pie, Penny fell asleep on her father's lap, and as he lifted her to his shoulder to carry her off to bed, she half opened her eyes.

"Tomorrow," Skip said, "you can come up to see the treehouse." Penny closed her eyes and was carried off to bed with the hint of a smile on her face.

CHAPTER VIII

Honest Mistake

Morning came late for the Chapmans the day after the storm. In fact, they were still lying around at 10:30 when the telephone rang. Skip went to answer it, licking his fingers as he went. Jim muttered over an antique magazine he held, "Hmm, phone's back on, can't say as I missed it."

Penny, finished with breakfast, was getting some bites and scratches attended to. "Mommie, are all the kitties okay?"

Shirley smiled "Well since I haven't even gotten dressed yet, I haven't been outside to check on them. They should be fine, but I'm sure they're very hungry."

"Boy! "Exclaimed Penny, "We never got up so late before!"

Skip returned to the table "True. But we never had a day like yesterday either." He helped himself to seconds. "That was Gramps. He said they're just starting to move around and he wanted us to know that the stuff he got at Langtry's sat in his trunk all night. He's going again after breakfast to replace it and into Barlow on some errands. Said to figure out if we need anything."

Did he say how Gramma was?" Jim and Shirley asked at the same time.

"Oh yeah, he said she's feeling much better. He's going to bring her here though, while he's gone."

Shirley laughed. "Probably can't make her stay down. Wonder what makes him think we can?"

Jim shook his head, "Can't be done."

Skip wiped his mouth as he jumped up. "Well, Dad, you said you'd come out and see the treehouse today. Are you ready?" he asked hopefully.

Mr. Chapman refilled his coffee cup as he said, "Sure am. Just let me have this last cup of coffee first."

"Okay," responded Skip as he gathered tools. "We'll go out and make sure it's all spruced up." He smiled at Penny who stood wide eyed, waiting to be sure she had really heard him invite her last night. Penny jumped up and they went out the screen door letting it bang and bounce and bang again.

Shirley and Jim sat in silence and watched the siblings run toward the orchard with Higby at their heels, barking happily. They looked at each other and shared thoughts without words. Then as Jim poured cream in his coffee, he commented, "Banging door, screeching little girl, barking dog … don't think anything's going to bother me today."

The kids wasted little time tidying the grounds around the treehouse. "Boy, I'm glad we came out ahead of Dad so we could get this mess cleared away." Skip said. Then he went up into the treehouse and pushed debris over the side for Penny to pull into the pile.

"There, that ought to do it" he announced finally as he brushed himself off.

"Now can I come up?" Penny pleaded, her head cocked sideways. "Ooh-kay." He teased, loving every moment of it, "but be careful." Skip coached her up rung by rung.

The treehouse sat braced by several upward branches and was supported by a huge forked branch that grew horizontally about 16 feet off the ground. It was a rectangular structure with a railed platform on the front. The roof was built to be peaked, and there were two framed window openings for the windows that Skip was going to install today. After that, he and his dad would shingle the plywood roof. Skip was explaining all this to Penny who sat Indian style in the middle of the room. She was holding a board that read 'THE HIDEWAY' that Skip had done with a wood burning tool.

"Anybody home?" called their father from below.

Skip stepped out onto the platform. "Come on up Dad! There's plenty of room."

Mr. Chapman came up, inspecting as he came. He stepped onto the landing. "Looks real good son, nice job on this platform." Skip was pleased as he showed his Dad into the main part of the treehouse. "Wonderful Skip, I'm really impressed!" He said proudly. As he started to lower himself down to sit beside Penny his eyes became fixed on the floor. He rubbed his fingers across the wood as Penny and Skip beamed with pride.

"Nice huh Dad?" Skip offered.

Mr. Chapman assessed the size of the floor. "I'll say it is, but"... clearing his throat, "Skip, where, uh"...he hesitated, "where did you get these planks?" He asked looking up at his son, his mouth hanging open.

"I told you, in the scrap pile in the barn. Remember I was talking about the nice wood Uncle Lawrence had in there?" Skip crouched down beside his father and thumped the floor with his knuckles. "Well this is it! Isn't it cool?"

Mr. Chapman was confused. "On the scrap pile or *near* it?" he prodded.

"On it Dad. Right after Penny fell. She knocked it wacky I guess because I never noticed them before then."

Skip was becoming concerned with all the questions. He watched his Dad study the wood and became nervous.

"How many boards was there Skip?" he asked tentatively, as though he really didn't want to know.

"Seven," Skip responded pensively. "Why Dad?"

"Oh boy" moaned Jim, at a loss for better words. "Bad news" he sighed, as he sat down. "These are the shelves out of the chiffierobe."

Penny gasped and put both hands over her mouth while Skip stammered "B...but Dad! Why did you put them there? I had no idea those were yours! You said the chiffierobe is in the tool shed!"

"I put them," his father spoke slowly, "on the workbench when Uncle Frank and I moved the monster. I hadn't taken time to go get them, and they were out of my way there, anyway. I really never dreamed they would get mixed up with scrap wood!"

"Oh m'gosh!" Skip slapped his forehead. "The workbench collapsed on one end. That's how Penny fell and got hurt that day."

Penny's face reddened. "I was trying to catch a bird Daddy and these boards musta fell off with me. I'm sorry Daddy. It's all my fault!" she exclaimed as her chin started quivering.

Mr. Chapman reached out and pulled Penny to his side. "Don't cry Penny, it won't help a bit and I'm not mad, really. Just disappointed, that's all. It was an honest mistake." He looked at Skip who appeared as though his world was about to collapse too. "Don't fret, Son. I told you that you could have any wood you found in the barn, as long as it was sturdy. "He appraised the floor in a new light. "The treehouse is turning out very nice pal," he said soberly, "and, well it's probably one of a kind. Who else has a hard maple floor in their treehouse? I'm sure some day we'll laugh at this, and you're sure to tell this story to your children and grandchildren but right now it's a little hard to be amused about it."

"Dad, I'll pull them up, today." Skip vowed.

Mr. Chapman stood, "No Skip, don't do that. There are nail holes all over now." He shook his head. "You can keep them. I'll finish the chiffierobe up and make shelves, someday. I just won't be able to enter it in the fair. He stood up slowly. "Know the worst part of it?" Neither Penny nor Skip ventured a guess. "My other project for this vacation was to paint the barn. Guess I'll have to start it now." He patted Skip's shoulder as he stepped out onto the platform and left the stunned children staring at the floor.

CHAPTER IX

The Stranger

The granite and sandstone pebbles that Penny had collected onto her lap fell to the ground when she was startled by the stranger's voice. She hadn't heard him approaching her in the yard and wouldn't have noticed him if he hadn't spoken.

"Good afternoon Missy. Oh, I'm sorry I surprised you."

"Hullo," she greeted tentatively. "Who are you?" He was even taller than her dad and had very large hands, Penny noticed, as she looked him over. He wore faded jeans and a tee shirt under his jean jacket. A straw hat shaded his straight brown hair and reddish beard. He smiled very nicely, Penny thought reminding her of a TV cowboy she liked.

"Well, I'm Stan. What's your name?" Penny paused and busied herself picking up the stones as she thought about talking to a stranger.

"Penny Chapman." she announced simply. "I'm seven and I got permoted to second grade, and I got Mr. Caskin for my new teacher. He's better'n Mrs. Willet. She's mean," Penny blurted, dismissing anything she had ever been taught about talking to strangers. She made a face at the man to demonstrate how mean Mrs. Willet is.

"Boy, I'll bet she is." He laughed at the animated little girl. "Tell me Penny, can I talk to your Dad or Mom?"

"Yup. Daddy's right over there." She leaned toward Stan and signaled him to take part in a secret. "He's paintin' the barn cause we wrecked his shelfsis."

"Oh, I see." He nodded even though he didn't know what it was she was talking about.

"Uh huh, we did and it's my fault." She crinkled up her face. Now I hafta go wash my stone c'lection. They got all dirty," she sighed.

"Okay and I'll go talk to your father," Stan said, as he knelt down and helped pick up the stones that kept slipping through Penny's fingers. "Here," he suggested, "put them in this," offering his hat.

Penny accepted the offer, dumped the treasures into his hat and took it from him. "Thank you, I'll give it back," she called back over her shoulder as she ran toward the pump. Stan headed for the barn.

Jim was high on a ladder painting the back of the barn when the stranger came around from the side and called up to him. "Mr. Chapman?"

Jim looked down and carefully placed the paintbrush on the paint can rim. "Yes Sir," he said, as he descended. "Jim," he added as he stepped down and offered his hand. "And you are?"

"Stan Southworth," Stan said as they shook. "Nice to meet you. Your daughter told me where I'd find you. Sorry to interrupt."

As if on cue both men looked up at his progress, admiring the few yards of bright white paint on the dull gray barn.

"No need to apologize, "Jim assured him, "I'm happy for the break. Besides, I'll be doing this for about two more weeks. I'm sure I can spare five minutes." He beckoned Stan to join him for ice water from a jug. "So what can I do for you?"

"Well, I'm not sure. You see, I'm in Barlow a few weeks early this year, because I work the fairs, and decided to pick up a temporary job here, 'til the County fair starts. We had a cancellation in Gibson because of the floods so I figured I'd just come ahead. I did have a job that lasted a week but it's done now, so I'm looking for something until the trucks start rolling in."

"Too bad about all the flooding, see any of it? Jim asked."

"Oh yeah! We had a three day wash out at Carmel too." He shrugged, "It happens. Midwestern weather is very unpredictable."

"That it is. We had a pretty nasty storm here last week." the painter added.

They walked into the shade.

"Some folks in town said to talk to the older people at the lake" Stan continued… "They hire things done. Then a fellow I've dealt with at the feed mill said I should to check with you first."

Jim nodded his head. "That would be my brother, Frank."
"Really?" Stan asked, surprised. "He didn't tell me that."

Jim nodded, smiling. "He's no talker, is he? Frank lives out at the lake and he's right. They're all busy every evening clearing away debris. You probably could pick up several little jobs. Fact is, had a big limb come down at my parent's place that we haven't cleared yet. Frank and I can get it though." He looked at Stan directly. "What do you do, generally?"

"For odd jobs? Anything. Even get in some haying, every so often. At the fairs, I'm foreman of the set and break crews and the rest of the time I maintain equipment and broker for supplies. Don't know if I'm considered a carnie…but that's how it all started."

Jim laughed, "Sounds a lot more adventuresome than accounting, Stan."

Stan shrugged. "Well, it's all I've ever known. Ran off when my Mother got married to a guy I didn't get on with and here I am, eighteen years later.

Not much to show for all those years. Send money back home. Guess that's about the only accomplishment I can claim. 'Course I have friends all over the place." He shrugged. "People who have hired me or just folks I've met in my travels. It's not a bad life."

"You are living every boy's dream, you know." Jim said appreciatively. The stranger laughed "Yeah, I know, 'course I'm not a boy anymore. Sure it sounds great but it's hot and dirty, the hours are crazy and I guess I'd have to say it gets lonely. I have a regular gang that works with me and we're pretty tight, but I want a family someday and some land."

Jim nodded. "Family is what makes the difference to me too. My wife and I both grew up here, went to the same school. Dad was on the school board; my cousin was our business teacher in high school. I've always enjoyed it, having my family around and a family of my own."

Stan smiled, enjoying the conversation.

Jim pretended to count on his fingers "Eighteen years of drifting. You might want to start looking pretty soon," he winked, "or is there someone?"

Stan shook his head and blushed. "Nope, not yet."

"On a different note, since that's none of my business," Jim apologized, "You ever work on a farm, repairing and painting? That kind of stuff?" Stan smiled broadly. "All the time."

"Well, this really isn't a working farm since I'm a city guy now. I have an accounting firm in Lincoln. So we just pack up and move down here every summer. I 'm off three weeks, then I commute on weekends. It's worth it, I love it here." He said, as he panned his hand across the property.

They surveyed the property as they drank. "It's real nice. I like farm country, like it a lot." Stan said reverently.

"Yeah," Jim agreed, "but I'd never make a living here, unfortunately." Jim wiped his forehead. "Stan," Jim interrupted his own speech, "I'd like to invite you for lunch and I'll go talk things over with my wife. There's plenty that needs attended to around here, including this barn and judging by the way my vacation is slipping by, I'm sure we can use you, but Shirley needs to agree. Come on in, we'll get lunch and talk some more."

"Thanks, Mr. Chapman...er Jim "Stan corrected himself. "First, I'll go up and close up that paint and take care of the brush." He nodded his head toward the drop cloth and spirits under the tree.

"Good deal!" Jim responded, encouraged by Stan's initiative. "Then come on up to the house and make yourself comfortable on the porch."

Stan met up with Penny again near the house and she introduced him to Higby. The friendly dog immediately located a tennis ball for a game of fetch.. "He's a watchdog ya'know." Penny informed the tall man.

Oh really. What does he watch?" Stan asked, tickled at the notion, considering Higby had greeted him earlier by licking his hand, when he entered the yard, and then went off to chase kittens."

Penny snickered. "He watches the ball silly!"

Shirley was in the den marking out a sundress pattern when Jim found her.

"Hey, you have enough help?" He smiled, motioning toward Snuff who was lying asleep in the middle of the table on the new fabric.

Shirley laughed, "Could be worse, Penny could be here too," she said, without looking up. "Who's the fella you were talking to? I saw him stop out front and thought maybe it was another one of Uncle Lawrence's workers from years gone by."

Jim shook his head. "No, his name is Stan Southworth. He works at the fair. He's well...ah....he a..."

Shirley stopped pinning and studied her husband, who wasn't given to hem-hawing, typically.

"He's a drifter, I suppose. Or a carnie. Or.... well if you'll just give him a chance," he scolded "you'll realize that he's a regular hardworking guy who has spent the last eighteen years of his life on the fair circuit!" he lectured.

"Jim!" She held up both hands, amused at his defensive outburst. "What is going on? I asked who he was. That's all."

"Oh. Oh yeah." Jim sat down quickly beside Shirley and spoke softly having heard Stan walk across the porch and sit in the creaky rocker.

CHAPTER X

Red Ears

As usual, Penny was the messenger who, along with Higby, ran for Skip when lunch was ready. "Figured it was about that time. Either I'm imagining it or we're having sweet corn for lunch and I can smell it clear out here." Skip chattered as he climbed down part way and jumped the rest of the way, landing upright near Penny with a thud.

"We *are* having corn on the cob!" shouted Penny astonished. Mommie got it in Barlow today." They began walking toward the house when Penny stopped suddenly and began sniffing the air. Her eyebrows were furrowed as she leaned first to the right and then to the left. She rolled her eyes dramatically as she sniffed for corn aroma, making tiny chugging sounds. Higby stopped and watched the curious actions and tipped his head left when she stretched left and right when she stretched right. Each time she rolled her eyes and sniffed, his tail twitched until he decided it was a game and began barking wildly and running in circles.

Skip watched, amused as Higby stopped in front of Penny and dropped to his front quarters. His backside stuck up in the air, his tail wagged double time. By this time it was Penny who was watching Higby. All at once after staring her down, Higby snorted, blowing the fine barnyard dust into his own eyes and nose. He batted his eyes and let out a ferocious sneeze rolling all the way over side-back-side and jumped to his feet. When he began the circling again, Skip and Penny laughed as they waved dust away from their faces.

"Higby! Here Boy." Skip chuckled as he leaned over and patted his jeans, "You better settle down, you're getting all steamed up."

"Aaaaaoooo" Penny wound down from laughing. "You're so funny, Higby. You should be on TV."

Lunch was quite an affair too with Skip describing Penny and Higby's antics and then Penny trying to explain why it seemed sensible to wash her stone collection *in* Stan's hat. "Well it has holes in it Daddy, don't you think it's for washing stuff?" she defended.

"Pen" … Jim sighed, at a loss for words.

Stan winked across the table at Penny. "She's right you know" he said in her defense.

Shirley surprised Jim, Stan and the kids when she announced that Stan was going to be staying with them for a while to help with the work. Jim figured she'd need a day or so to think about it and the kids just thought he was a visitor.

"I want the two of you", she looked at Skip and Penny, "to help me get the bedroom behind the den ready this afternoon."

Jim smiled at Stan. "Guess it's settled. We'll talk about details while we set up a scaffold." Jim said with a new enthusiasm.

"Sure enough," he nodded to Jim. Thanks to you both. 'Specially you Mrs. Chapman, I'll be another one to cook for."

"Shirley", she smiled.

Penny stared at the new friend quizzically. "Where's your pajamas at Stan? Don't you wear pajamas? My brother don't, he sleeps in his underw…" Her words suddenly stopped and were held firmly in her mouth by Skip who grabbed her head with both hands, and grimaced as his ears turned red.

"Dad!" he pleaded as he let his bug-eyed sister go.

Jim tapped his finger on the table soundly beside Penny's plate of half eaten food. She buttoned her lips. "Okaeee." She said, fully aware that Dad's finger on the table meant *no more talking*.

Stan leaned over to Skip, who was still embarrassed about such personal information being given to a stranger, and whispered. "Pajamas...who needs 'em?" Skip mustered a smile and continued eating.

The only talk directed to Penny for the rest of the meal was "Wipe off your chin" and "Finish your milk." Finally, exasperated, she stood up. "Es-kuze me." She stomped to the door. "Stan can I talk to you later?," she asked emphatically as she glared at the family, "In pri-vit!"

Stan covered his mouth with his napkin to hide his smile. "Yes Ma'am, you certainly may", he muffled.

"C'mon Higby," she ordered, and marched out the door, letting it slam just within the law.

CHAPTER XI

Lucky Break

Skip was up and dressed in 'real' clothes before breakfast. For one thing, he had on socks which were defiantly not a part of his summer attire. He wore chinos and his newest polo with the green collar. When he arrived at the table he was greeted by hoots and whistles. About the same time things settled down from Skip's surprise debut, Penny paraded in wearing the new yellow sundress her mother had sewn; white sandals and she carried her white purse. But she was pouting.

"I wanted to surprise you," she muttered down the front of her dress.

Jim got up and swept her into his arms. "You did One Cent," a nickname reserved for special occasions, "you both did. What's going on?" he asked.

"Gramps and Gramma are taking us somewhere" Skip offered. Penny took her dad's face in her hands "It's a surprise for you."

Skip shot a glance at Penny. "Yeah. We don't even know where we're going." He looked sternly at his sister. "But I don't know what is the matter with her. Probably wanted to come down before I did and make a big entrance."

They all looked at her.

"What'sa matter is this!" she blurted, turning her head for all to see her ponytails cockeyed and scarcely holding with wisps of hair sticking everywhere.

"Oh that, I barely noticed." Jim lied. "Mom will just need to tighten things up a little." He assured her.

Skip was able to keep from laughing but he and Stan exchanged secret grins. "Don't feel bad Penny, Mom was still combing my hair when I started fifth grade," encouraged Skip.

"She still ties my ties once in a while." Jim added as he watched Shirley redo Penny's hair. Shirley laughed out loud.

"And I pick out his clothes and match his socks." Jim blushed but took the poking good naturedly.

Hair repair completed, breakfast over and joking aside, Penny and Skip were ready when they heard Grampa toot in the driveway.

When the children left, the three adults finished a pot of coffee and Shirley began clearing the table.

"Hey maw" Jim bellowed "chillins is out fer the day, whataya say we pull out the cards and play blackjack?"

"Better idea Paw, chillins out fer the day, let's haul out the lye soap an scrub down the chuck wagin, here." Shirley responded. Highly amused with themselves, they looked to Stan for his contribution. He stammered and held up his hands.

"Hold on pardners. Where I come from...ya don't work...ya don't eat. I got chores to do!" He got up to leave.

"See y'all" he said as he tossed on his 'c'llection hat.'

Jim jumped up and was right behind him. "I ain't gittin' held hostage in here! "S'long Cookie." he called back as he left.

Skip sat in Pete and Sally's kitchen trying to recall when he had been there before. The whole room seemed a faint memory but it was the mingled smells that brought him to realize that he must have visited this place a long time ago. There was the aroma of fresh baked bread, he would recognize that smell anywhere, and coal. He recognized the scent of coal. Uncle Lawrence's farmhouse used to have a coal burning furnace and bin too, Skip remembered with a smile. He recalled how that first year he and Penny climbed through the coal pile and found shiny gold tinfoil "treasures" with "secret codes" from the coal yard. Skip smiled at the people engaged in conversation, but his mind continued to go back in his childhood. He revisited the fun he and Penny had out behind the farmhouse house trying to build sculptures with the gray clinkers. Then he recalled his utter dismay when his Dad said that he had ordered a new furnace for the farmhouse and said flatly, "when the coal is gone, so goes the furnace."

Guess Uncle Pete still uses a coal furnace, he thought as he returned to the here and now. He watched his great Uncle for a moment and then suddenly placed him because of the hair growing out in silver tufts from his ears. That had made an impression on him years ago when he asked Uncle Pete why he grew hair there. He vividly remembered the aged uncle telling him it was troll hair. Skip needed lots of convincing that evening when he told his parents the worrisome information. Now, as Skip watched him, he had to laugh at himself and admire the old guy for pulling one over on him. Skip didn't really recognize Aunt Sally though. "Sally hasn't been well until recently," Gramma told the kids on the ride over. She also helped Skip and Penny make the family connections. "Uncle Pete is my brother. Uncle Lawrence, who gave your Mom the farm, was another brother. I had four brothers; Pete is the only one living."

Penny didn't know anyone in the kitchen but was wasting no time getting acquainted with Inez, the elderly couple's daughter, who seemed to Skip to be sixty plus herself.

"Last we seen of that chiffierobe Wilma" drawled Pete, "was when Nez come back home and cleant out the upstairs for her apartment. She got rid of 'bout everthing, dint ya 'Nezzie?

The woman nodded as she held Penny close to her side. "Sure did, I sold a lot of things, and got enough to pay Dad's taxes and get the house worked on." She laughed. "Of course we did get rid of a lot of stuff too but that piece and some ladder back chairs, I think, went to the high school. Hal Wade was moving my belongings in and asked what was going to become of the chiffierobe and the chairs. He wanted them for his senior shop class. I know they had a course in furniture history and restoration. I can't say as he still has them though, because the school's in a building program now. Plus I retired right before I moved in with Ma and Dad." Then she offered, "I could probably find out though, with a quick phone call."

Gramma smiled "We would sure appreciate it Inez. It would be wonderful if we could get those replacement shelves for Jim." Inez got up and went to the parlor to make the phone call.

Sally poured milk and coffee for her guests and sliced a loaf of nut bread. She drizzled cinnamon syrup on a piece and handed it to Penny. "Sure is nice to see you Wilma and Carl." And then she pointed to the kids, and raised her soft voice. "Peter do you believe this is the same little Skip and tiny Penny that were here few years back?"

Pete shook his head slowly, thinking back "Shore don't seem possible does it Sal?"

The groups exchanged talk about their families and were engaged in a lively conversation with Penny about her boat experience when they were interrupted by Inez who came in saying "Keep your fingers crossed kids. Hal was on vacation so I called Mr. Osborne, the principal. He said he thinks the chiffierobe is still out in the shop storing paint. He said he's planning to be at the school tomorrow to meet with the heating contractor, and he'll be available about ten o'clock if you want to come look at it. He said if it fills the bill, you can have it. They will be moving into the new commercial arts building in the next few weeks and won't be taking any of the old stuff." Inez smiled as Gramma clapped her hands together, and said "That's just what we'll do!"

Penny hugged Inez. "Daddy will be so happy!"

CHAPTER XII

Secret Mission

Gramma entered the kitchen first, carrying a plate of hot sticky buns and Gramps followed with a quart of blueberries. "Coffee ready Shirley?" Gramps asked hopefully.

"Sure is Dad, here let me take those, I'm ready for them. Help yourself to coffee. Jim and the kids should be down soon." She poured batter on the griddle. "Stan is outside already, moving ladders."

"How's he working out, Shirley?" asked her mother-in-law as she started setting the table.

Shirley shrugged and said, "Fine. Jim has really been happy to have him around, they get along very well and apparently he's an excellent worker. "She looked at her in-laws. "Just as important, he's as pleasant as can be and the kids love him."

Carl returned the coffee pot and said, "That's great. I like him too, but we were both a little concerned when he drifted in and Jim hired him, on the spot. You never know these days. There are plenty of smooth talkers out there."

"Oh I know." She agreed. "Jim and I had some concerns but both felt he deserved a chance. Plus, Jim called Frank and Frank remembers selling feed to him at past fairs. Frank said for years."

Their discussion was cut short by Skip thumpity thumping down the steps. "Hi Gramps! Hi Gramma!" Skip greeted "Umm what smells so good?" he asked as he began peeking under napkins and pot lids. "Blueberry pancakes and sticky buns! Wow! What's the occasion?" he asked enthusiastically.

"Nothing really, just happens this way sometimes." said Shirley, as she handed him a pitcher of syrup.

"Boy, I wish we could eat together everyday!" he exclaimed as he landed in a chair.

Stan had come in and was chatting with Gramps when Jim and Penny arrived noisily from upstairs. "Let's eat!" Shirley announced.

"Think we can finish up the barn today Stan?" Jim asked hopefully as he polished off his stack of pancakes.

Stan wiped his whiskers, picked up his coffee and walked to the window. "Don't see why not, if the weather holds and we put in a pretty good day. Especially with your help on the trim, Mr. Chapman."

Gramps nodded. "I have always enjoyed doing the trim work. Sort of like decorating a cake. Really finishes a paint job off."

Jim mouthed a yuck to Stan behind his father's back.

Shirley, who was already clearing away dishes with Gramma, patted Jim's shoulder. "Are you sure you don't need us home in time for lunch?"

"Naw! Go ahead and shop. I'm sure we can make some sandwiches by ourselves," he assured. Penny's eyes widened when she heard her dad say they were going shopping. She waited for the conversation to lag, so she could set him straight, but her grandmother, sensing it, shushed her quietly.

"Well of course we can. Fact is I make lunch 'bout every day at home, don't I Granny?" Gramps added.

"He sure does," she smiled, "and I clean up the mess."

Carl dropped his mouth open in utter surprise and looked toward the window. "Hem…" he said, "think we better get out ahead of the heat boys?"

Stan and Jim rose together. "Think the heats already on you Dad," Jim laughed.

After the men left, those remaining sat around the table and went over their "shopping" plans.

"Skip, you measured the chiffierobe again, didn't you?" asked Gramma. Skip nodded "Yup. Dad didn't see me either."

"Okay," Shirley said as she tossed a towel to the drainer. "Let's head out to the school."

"I sure hope this works out," worried Skip "it just seems too far fetched that we could actually find a match for Dad's chiffierobe."

"Well maybe so," Shirley agreed "but how would we know if we don't try? Besides, Gramps says it *is* a match.

"Then it is." added Penny. "My Grampa knows everything!"

"Ha!" Wilma said as she smiled at Shirley.

"Must be how Jim got so smart don't you suppose?" Shirley added.

CHAPTER XIII

Sad Discovery

Mr. Osborne came out of the gymnasium door just in time to help Shirley Chapman lift Penny off a sticky tar patch in the parking lot.

"Did you have to step in that Penny?" she asked impatiently.

"Here," Mr. Osborne offered. "Let me carry you over to the building Little Lady, your feet might get burned."

Skip tugged the sticky flip flop from the tar where it stuck and Shirley took the other from Penny's foot. "Here Skip," she instructed, "might as well toss them in that incinerator. They'll never clean up." Gramma had gone ahead with the principal and was explaining to him how they ran down the chiffierobe. Penny looked back at Skip as she cruised at six feet, partly in embarrassment and partly as if to say, "Well just look at me, being carried by a real Principal."

When Skip and Shirley caught up, Wilma introduced the family. Mr. Osborne clapped Skip on his shoulder." Bet you're anxious to straighten this out, aren't you son?

"Skip blushed, "Sure am. I really screwed up this time."

"Sure did." Agreed Penny. Skip looked at her in disgust. "I...I mean I did too." Mr. Osborne looked at them sympathetically. His hard soled shoes made a clicking sound on the shiny hallway floor. Skip flip-flopped in beat and Penny's bare feet made little slapping sounds, double time. The two ladies leather sandals occasionally squeaked and Penny was thoroughly enjoying the foot concert as they progressed down the long halls.

"My! The school looks so nice," Gramma complimented.

"It sure does," said Mr. Osborne, turning to them as they walked. "Takes a good sized crew about two to three weeks to get the painting, stripping and waxing done." He smiled at Penny and Skip. "And it takes the students only about one week to get it back to normal."

"Inez said your new wing is about ready." Shirley commented.

"That it is," Mr. Osborne agreed with obvious relief. "Still, I think we'll have construction crews here, tying up loose ends even after school starts. But" he added, "in addition to the new shop, we'll have brand new art department facilities and a room and office for the newspaper and another separate one for the yearbook. It's a wonderful improvement." The group rounded a corner and Mr. Osborne said, "Here we are," as he sorted through a large ring of keys and unlocked the door to the old shop. While he pulled the door open for them and ushered them in, he continued.

"This will become the agricul...." His words died on his lips as he stood and stared at the vast expanse of the room. The two story high concrete and steel room was empty except for a few small cartons of cleaning supplies and a neat group of desks near the door where they stood. Across the room in the opposite corner stood the chiffierobe. His puzzled guests were focusing more on him, however, waiting to hear what he was concerned about.

"Is there something wrong, Mr. Osborne?" Shirley inquired.

"I don't believe this," he answered weakly. There's something wrong, all right, something very wrong." He pressed his hands against his temples, looked around as though he was working through a problem in his mind. Finally he made a fist and pounded at an invisible bench as if to announce he had reached a conclusion. He turned to the group, staring at them with a dull expression. Most of the color had drained from his face. "We've been robbed." he announced simply.

"What's missing?" asked Skip after a polite pause. He tried to sound concerned but not give it away that he was excited about being in on the literal ground floor of a mystery.

"Equipment" responded the Principal. Thousands of dollars worth of equipment for the new shop and art departments. Lathes, bench saws and power miters. And the press!" He realized. "There was a press for the journalism classes. They were all still in shipping crates," he said in unbelief.

"Maybe the builders have already moved the equipment in to the new building," reasoned Wilma.

He shook his head and looked at the women. "I was just over there; it's not ready. We figured about ten days." He squeezed the key ring and rubbed it on his chin. "This is horrible," he said softly, looking at them but his mind was elsewhere. "Listen folks, there's the chiffierobe. You go ahead and look it over, but please don't touch anything. I have to go notify the sheriff." He looked around again and left.

The party stood stunned, staring blankly at each other. That is except for Skip, who was starting to walk around with his hands firmly clasped behind his back to remind him not to touch anything. "Fingerprints. That's what they want," he told Penny.

Penny shivered from head to toe and her grandmother pulled her close to her body. "Don't be afraid, Penny," she comforted.

Penny looked up at her. "I'm not scared Gramma. I'm cold. This c'ment feels wet."

Skip pointed high up to a window that was missing a large pane. "Probably got wet from the change in temperature. It's condensation. Here," Skip slipped off his flip flops and slid them toward Penny. "You can use them. My feet never get cold," he said importantly.

Shirley and Penny thanked Skip, and then Shirley said, "Well," trying to reorganize her thoughts, "the chiffierobe." They walked to it quickly. There were signs of amateur refinishing efforts on the lower half that looked like test patches. The door on the left hung crooked having lost several screws in the hinges. The right door was missing entirely.

"Look! The shelves," Skip said earnestly, being careful not to touch them. "Seven you guys. They're all here. Looks like the exact same thing." He grinned.

Shirley and Gramma bent and examined the plate on the floor of the closet "It is. Here's the plate." Shirley affirmed. It read: Trimble Bros. of Andersonville Model 437-F 1887. Skip stepped closer and studied the blackened brass plate. He looked up at his mother and grandmother and smiled.

"We did it! Penny screeched as she jumped up and down clumsily in Skip's flip-flops.

"The shelves are in nice shape," Shirley pointed out to Wilma. "Just a paint ring or two, but I don't see any deep marring."

Gramma took Penny's hand and her expression turned serious. "Looks like our little bit of detective work turned out well for us. We were very lucky. I only hope Mr. Osborne will be so fortunate. He has to be devastated," she said sadly.

Skip resumed his tour of the room and then returned to the group. "Yeah.

Our lucky day turns out to be his unlucky day." They turned when they heard Mr. Osborne enter the room.

"They're on their way" he said grimly. "You know I was thinking" addressing the women "if it hadn't been for that old chiffierobe, we might not have discovered this for another week or two."

"I'm not so sure about it being helpful" Shirley disagreed. "Looks to me like this chiffierobe played a part in the robbery." She pointed as she talked. "Look how it's under the open window. It's been moved, see the scrape marks?"

"I see them alright" said Mr. Osborne, but the only part the chiffierobe may have played in this burglary is for the last thief to get out. The theft took place through that shipping door." They all turned toward the end of the building that faced the staff parking lot. "That's the loading dock", he explained "and whoever took the contents of this room had a big truck and a forklift. The press alone weighs over two ton. "Skip brightened "There's lots of tracks, Mr. Osborne."

"There would have to be" he responded, nodding his head. "The most troublesome thing about this, to me, is there are so many possibilities. It had to be an inside job. The control for that door lock is over there and calls for a special key. Those keys are in my office and on this key ring." He rattled the keys as he addressed the women. "We've had construction crews, maintenance crews, architects, and of course the school board walking through much of the building all summer long. All the foremen had keys to the areas they had to be in." He heaved a sigh, "I'm afraid this is going to be a long drawn out affair." The group nodded in agreement. "Which reminds me," he added, "I need to call my wife. We were leaving for Sarasota in the morning. We have a new grandson," He smiled thoughtfully. 'Never have seen him. I've had to be here all summer to be sure everything was going along okay. Lot of good that did, huh?"

"Oh what a shame." Wilma sympathized, "double disappointment." Everyone turned when they heard footsteps down the hall.

"Well, this is it, the sheriff is here. By the way, what about the chiffierobe?" he asked.

Wilma smiled. "It's exactly what we need."

"Great! I'm genuinely happy for you," he assured them.

Sheriff Lansing and two officers entered the room and approached the group. They were all introduced and the deputy took Wilma and Shirley's names and telephone numbers.

As he walked them to the door, Mr. Osborne assured them he'd call as soon as possible so Frank could pick up the chiffierobe. "For now, "he said, "everything needs to be the way we found it."

CHAPTER XIV

Confusion

Jim Chapman was all smiles as he sat at the picnic table with Shirley, his mother and Skip. "What a day! First we get the barn done over a week ahead of when I would have, largely thanks to those two fellas over there. "he motioned to Stan and Carl Sr. who were drinking at the pump. He turned and tussled Skip's hair. "Then you tell me you've found replacement shelves. How in the world did you find an exact match that someone would give up?"

"Gramma's brother" announced Penny, climbing onto the bench on her father's other side.

"Uncle Pete?"

"Yup. 'Ness did it," confirmed the elated little girl. "She gave it to Mr. Osmond and he gave it to us!"

"Ness? Mr. Osmond?" He tried to place them but couldn't.

"Inez," clarified Gramma. "Cousin Inez."

"Ah ha!" He said as he winked at Shirley. "I still think of her as Miss Carlson. She was also our teacher," he explained to the kids. "How's she doing anyway? I haven't seen her for a long time."

"Well we hadn't either, since she traveled summers and taught through the school year, but she's retired now. Sold her home and put in an apartment at Pete and Sally's."

"Really!" he said, surprised. Wilma laughed. "Surprised me too, but when you think of it, she couldn't have moved them in to her small home and they really need her."

Skip was watching Gramps and Stan toss horseshoes but he was going through his grandmother's genealogy lesson, from two days ago, in his mind. "Mom, I thought Uncle Lawrence was your Uncle."

Shirley smiled. "He was."

"And Uncle Pete is his brother?"

Then Skip turned to his father. "Inez is *your* cousin? "he confirmed.

"Uh huh."

"Your cousin's father is Mom's Uncle? You know Mom, this is way worse than Dad, Gramps and I having the same name!"

"Did you ever hear about kissing cousins Skip?" Jim teased. "That's Mom and me!" he announced proudly.

Skip nearly fell off the bench. "Oh my gosh Dad!"

"James Chapman!" scolded Wilma, "don't upset that boy."

Jim kept laughing and Penny started in too, not needing to know why. Carl wandered over and Stan pulled out of the driveway.

"Okay, I'll help you out, since Dad is out of control here," offered Shirley.

"You see my Uncle Lawrence and Aunt Leah pretty much raised me. Aunt Leah passed away before you were born. I remember her though, very fondly. Her brother Albert is my father. Albert Taylor. I barely remember him. My mother Julia Taylor worked all the time and I grew up, basically, at Aunt Leah and Uncle Lawrence's. They were my family. Uncle Pete and Uncle Lawrence are Gramma's brothers. That's how I came to know Dad when we were children.

"Oh, okay, I see…er I think. It's kinda confusing, but, well it's just that…," he paused, knitting his brows tightly and then began again thoughtfully." When we first moved here, you know, that first summer? Hatch's dad told me not to "go getting hitched with a cousin," then he pointed at me and laughed his head off." Skip paused and scratched his arm, nervously. "So I guess I kinda been, well sorta worried that my friends in Lincoln were making fun, you know behind my back, like we're all hicks or something." He looked at his mother, feeling the red coming into his cheeks. "Now you tell me this."

Jim picked up on Skip's serious tone and settled in to listen to his son.

Penny wandered away.

Stan was on his way to the fire hall to pick up carryout for everyone from the fish fry, prompting Shirley to tease, "Is this because you want to celebrate finishing the barn, or don't you guys want us to see the kitchen?"

Gramps slid in beside Gramma as they listened to Skip's rare confession. All four of them worked at going through the families by name again but decided, since Skip couldn't put faces together with names, to wait until the reunion when the families all gathered together at the fair.

Gramps helped Skip the most by putting things into perspective. "Skip," he said "this old community is made up of many large families such as ours. Families used to be very large and they all stayed around. Just think of all the aunts and uncles and cousins," he suggested.

"And grandparents "Wilma added. Grampa and I, your great grandma Harper, Grampa's parents Grampa John and Gramma Carla. You have a nice big family. I think it's important to realize that they are *your* family, too, "she added.

"Yeah, they are aren't they? Guess I always have thought of them as Dad's family or Mom's."

Gramps continued, "Around here with this being a farming community, the families used to stay in tact because everyone is needed to keep a farm going. Two, three generations sometimes, working together. That is what makes outsiders think we're all related to each other. In a sense we are, because large families produce many new families. They spread out for miles, working the land."

"Know what?" Skip asked suddenly

"What?" they chorused.

"Sometimes, I wish we lived here year round. I mean, I like our home in Lincoln a lot and my friends and all that stuff, but out here it's ...different. Everyone knows you Gramps, or Gramma and, lots of people are realizing that we're Chapmans too. People take time to talk to you or help you. Look how Mr. Osborne helped us...and well, I don't know. It's neat."

Jim slapped Skip on the back. "That's why we're back here every chance we get. We live in Lincoln because I am an accountant and there is already an accounting firm in Barlow. And the Chapman Mill couldn't support us and Uncle Frank's family, too, because of the economy. There isn't enough business. That's also why your great uncles sold out their farms."

Gramma added "But the family's ties are as strong as ever. That's why we look forward to reunion."

"Think you understand things better now?" Shirley asked.

"Yeah, for now anyhow, and I was just thinking. Mr. Hatcher doesn't have any business teasing me. He's not even married anymore and his kids leave for their mom's every single Friday at 5 o'clock. What does he know about family?"

Jim shook his head. "Skip that's probably the best arrangement they could make. They are still a family. Anybody can be a family...ours is just a country mouse-city mouse type of family." Shirley shook her head in agreement

"Maybe you should have Hatch down sometime." Shirley suggested.

Skip agreed, eagerly. "I will."

He thought for a minute. "Mom?"

"Yes son?"

"I know your mother is buried at the cemetery in Barlow, but where is Grampa Taylor buried?" He looked up at Shirley.

Shirley thought for a moment about her father as Jim leaned over and kissed her gently on the forehead.

"Only in my mind Skip. He's still alive; I think," she said softly.

Skip opened his mouth to ask a question but nothing came to him. He just cleared his throat.

"Stan's heeere!" bellowed Penny from the air two feet above the ground as she flew from her swing.

Skip turned but didn't miss the melancholy look on his mother's face.

CHAPTER XV

Suspicion

The group chatted about the chiffierobe over their fish dinners at the picnic table. Penny began rambling confidently, starting with the trip across the parking lot, the foot noises down the hall and a lengthy description of the room. But when she arrived at the matter at hand, she simply announced, "Mr. Osmond said you can't have the fingerprints so you just hafta wait, Daddy."

Jim looked at her, befuddled, after replaying what she just said in his head.

Shirley and Wilma got up and Shirley said, "Good Luck, Daddy" and left with the silverware and table cloth. "Let's go make some coffee, Mom. I think they're going to need it."

Jim watched amazed as his wide eyed daughter nodded her head consolingly.

"Mr. Osmond. He's the principal right?" Jim asked her. "And the chiffierobe has prints on it? I'm just getting sketches here."

Penny nodded her head in little bobbing shakes and stared at her dad with her lips pursed.

"I'll tell you the whole story Dad," Skip offered. "First off, it's Mr. Osborne not Osmond. Anyway, he took us to the old shop to let us check out the chiffierobe that the shop teacher got from Inez, well actually from Uncle Pete's place. But when he, Mr.

Osborne, unlocked the room at the school, the equipment for the new building was gone."

"Got robbed right out of there Daddy!" interrupted Penny. "He called the p'leece. But he told Gramma it was a in-the-door job, and they used the big one so now he has to stay off his vacation again!"

"Ohhhhh Penny! You're wearing me out." Jim protested mockingly.

Stan walked up and jumped in to the confusion by saying, "Mr. Osborne at Barlow High School?"

"Yeah," Skip answered. "Didn't you hear us before?"

Stan shrugged, "Guess I must have missed something. I heard Shirley tell you that they got shelves or something?"

"Right," Skip confirmed "but didn't you hear about the robbery part?" "There was a robbery?" Stan asked, stiffening his back.

Penny popped up from hanging upside down on the bench. "In the chiffienboard room." And then she disappeared again.

"Penny!"

"Yes Daddy," she answered obediently from under the table. "I know, *no more talking.*"

Stan smacked the table. "That's where I saw a chiffierobe like yours, in the shop!"

The whole group looked at him, including Penny who nearly burst due to her talking ban.

He quickly added, "I was in there when we waxed the floors. That's where I worked."

"Uh oh Stan," remarked Skip. "You're a suspect. Mr. Osborne said everyone who worked there this summer was. He said he was sure it was an inside job."

Jim laughed out loud. "It's not funny, I know, but was that what Penny meant about the big in-the-door job?"

"She meant inside job Dad and mixed that up with what Mr. Osborne said about them using the service door," Skip explained.

"The big one," Jim translated aloud.

Penny climbed out from under the table onto Gramps' lap. "That's what I said, Skip! You think you're so smart with your 'fisticated words," she blasted.

Skip looked at Penny and at the three smiling men and said, "I'm too tired for this,"and walked away, shaking his head.

Later in the week Skip came out to the tool shop where Jim was working on the chiffierobe. He had Penny's sandals that they had bought to replace the flip flops she ruined the day they went to the high school.

"Hi Dad. Don't you have that done yet?" he teased.

Jim looked up from his work. "Almost Skip. If I work on it every day for a week I should have it ready. Trouble is I only have three days of my vacation left."

"Oh that's right," Skip recalled sadly. "Anything I can do to help?" Jim laughed warmly "No Skip, you've done enough already." Skip dropped his head.

"Come on Skip, back at me! It's okay, I was teasing." He looked at the sandals. "What are you doing with those?"

"I almost forgot. Mom wants you to put holes half an inch up the strap. They're too loose."

"Nothing to it." He took the sandals over to the workbench and located a punch. As he measured and put in the holes he remembered why Penny had gotten yet another pair of sandals "Your sister is one of a kind, I tell you. 'Course I really don't need to tell you that do I?"

When Skip failed to answer, Jim turned to face his son's back. "Skip, where are you?"

'Oh, sorry Dad. Just thinking.'" Skip stepped out the door then back in and closed it. "Dad, where is Stan?"

"He went to the fairgrounds to get some things started. Why?"

Skip walked over to the chiffierobe and rubbed the new finish. "I don't know. I just think that it's funny that Stan didn't know about the robbery, and yet, he was there in that very room and the reason he gave was that he was waxing the floors."

Jim stopped and watched Skip closely. "I don't see anything wrong with that. He told me he had worked in the area; I never thought it was important to know where he worked. He's a hired hand. Nearly every farm around here hires workers at some time or another." Jim opened a drawer and dropped his awl into it "Besides, you said yourself that the school was freshly painted and the floors waxed."

"Right, I did but I didn't say *that* room was painted or waxed. The floor is concrete Dad. I know because Penny was barefoot and said it was cold and wet."

Jim wrinkled his brow. "Well, I don't think that necessarily means anything. He may have just passed by there or ...well any number of things could have taken place. "He reasoned "I don't know, Stan seems to be a real regular guy and I really don't think he has any more idea about what might have happened than we do." He shook his head doubtfully. "I guess we should keep our eyes and ears open though." He paused. "You do know that the sheriff talked to him yesterday don't you?"

Skip nodded. "Yeah, and I heard him tell Stan that he may need to talk to him again Dad. I figured it was because he was a stranger. Like it or not," Skip continued seriously, "he hasn't been cleared."

Jim conceded with a nod as he pulled the light chain and clicked the swinging bulb off. Let's be very careful about this Skip, I don't want to stir up any concern here and I especially wouldn't want Penny to get wind of anything. She could say the wrong thing and do some definite damage."

"I guess you're right," Skip agreed. "I know I wouldn't want to hurt Stan, I really like him. I just hope he's wasn't involved."

"I'll second that" Jim offered, "especially since he lives right here in the house with us. And for that matter, he has our van right now."

As they approached the house Jim raised his voice, "So where is that Cinderella gal? I want to try this slipper on her!"

Skip shook his head and rolled his eyes at his dad. "I'll be right back; I want to see if the Patriot is in the mailbox"

Skip walked down the drive slowly, reading the weekly paper. He was disappointed with the short report on the school theft and quickly switched his attention to the fair supplement that was inserted in this week's issue.

"There! How's that Cinderella Chapman?" asked Jim as he buckled the second sandal.

"Just right!" Penny announced as she marched around the kitchen. "Now can we go to Aunt Betty's, Mommie, please?"

Shirley looked up from pouring coffee. "Oh, I think we'll wait a little while, it's still pretty early."

Penny slumped to the floor and whined "I been waitin' all day already." She accepted a sympathetic kiss from Higby.

Shirley smiled "its twenty minutes 'til ten, Penny, so Aunt Betty hasn't even left the mill yet. We'll leave at ten." She looked at Jim. "Betty says a new family moved into the Rogers home next to them and they have two girls, so Penny is anxious to go meet them."

Jim smiled at the little girl-dog heap. "Sounds like a good idea, no one here to play with."

Penny looked up shaking her finger "'Cep for Higby and Snuff but they can't talk and they don't play nice together, 'cause I think," she said softly, covering Higby's ears, "they're both jellyus to each other."

Jim nodded agreeably. "Me too, I think they're very jealous."

Skip came in the door scooting an assortment of kittens away from the entrance. "Cats are hungry Pen," he suggested absently.

"That's right honey, go feed them and check Higby's water and then we'll go," directed her mother.

Skip handed the paper to his dad and held up the booklet he was reading. "Barlow County Fair Bulletin came with it, too." He said as he sat down to read.

Jim and Shirley sat side by side and combed the article about the robbery.

"Seems like you got more information out of Mr. Osborne than this reporter did. No mention of the method used or anything", said Mr. Chapman.

Shirley got up and gathered the cups, and said, "Nothing we didn't already know, except for the specifics on the equipment that was taken."

Skip looked up from his reading. "Guess Mr. Osborne didn't want to tip anyone off."

Jim leaned into Skip. "You know really Skip, this is a crime that goes way beyond Barlow. It involves state funding. The school has to do whatever the investigators say and I'm sure that they have told Mr. Osborne to keep it very quiet and low key. After all it's all guesswork right now."

CHAPTER XVI

Sisters

Penny stood and watched the sisters down on the lakeshore for several minutes before she worked up enough courage to go down to meet them. The older one was tall, about as tall as Skip. She had dark hair, tied up in ponytails. Penny smiled with satisfaction, knowing she had something in common with her already and they hadn't even met. The pony tailed one was busy on the beach raking the sandy soil for stones and debris.

The smaller girl was talking to the older girl as she walked away from her to the lawn trailer to dump her basket. The littler one followed her along the grass at the edge of the beach talking the whole time. Penny had no idea what she was talking about, but she could hear sounds and they all came from the smaller girl. When they turned to come back even closer toward Frank and Betty's lot, Penny was taken by the younger girl's blond hair and pretty features.

As Penny moved slowly down the hill toward the girls, she found herself straightening her bangs and brushing at her clothes. The blond girl was dressed up Sunday best, and Penny felt just a little underdressed. Penny continued timidly down the hill not entirely sure why she was so nervous. Boy, she thought, that blond girl sure is fancy.

She reached Aunt Betty's dock and walked along the lake, looking at the watery bubbles in the sand where the lake softly lapped and ebbed.

"Hey little kid!"

Penny jumped at the harsh words.

"This is private property!"

"Sondra, hush. Can't you see she's coming over to meet us?" The older girl straightened up and brushed her hands on her cut off jeans. She approached Penny. "Hi. You live around here?"

Penny liked the big one instantly but stammered because of the cold stare of the sister who stood statue like on the grass. "Huh-lo, I…um live on Lake Road." She fixed her eyes on the smiling girl who was greeting her. "My Aunt Betty and Uncle Frank live here." She began to relax and continued, "Grampa and Gramma too…right over there." She pointed out the cottage.

"The gray one?" The big girl asked.

"Yup" she said as she ventured a curious smile toward the other, stiffly posed girl, who felt pressured to speak.

"Hello," she said curtly "I'm Sondra Burroughs." Stepping forward, she gestured toward her sister, "This is my sister Antoinette. We've just come here this week. That's our new summer cottage."

Penny glanced up the slope at the sprawling home with decks built out on the hillside tying the home into the lake shore.

"We also have a home in Winnetka and a travel home that we take to Tahoe every year." Sondra waited for the announcement to sink in, but Penny just stood on the beach and waited for something to come out of her own mouth.

Penny began to feel uneasy with the pause when Antoinette took the lead. "Don't listen to Sondra, she's a snob." Penny started feeling like her old self.

"I thought so." she said honestly.

Antoinette laughed. "What's your name?" "Penny Chapman." Penny said shyly, I'm seven."

Sondra approached her. "Penny your real name," she asked, not hiding her boredom.

"Nope."

"Well what's your proper name?"

"Penelope Ann Chapman."

"Really. I've never heard of a name like that," Sondra added distastefully. Penny shifted and broke eye contact with Sondra for the comfort of a smile from Antoinette. Still she felt herself blushing as she defended herself. "It's my Great Gramma Harper's name. She didn't need it any more. I like Penny best though." She brightened. "Is Sandra your really name?"

"It's not Sandra; it's Sondra. I hate it when people call me by the wrong name! Sondra Elizabeth Burroughs, that's my proper name, "she scolded. She ended her tirade with her nose stuck in the air.

Penny was speechless again and on the verge of retreat.

Antoinette shook her head and looked at Penny. "You can call me Toni. I don't much like fancy names myself."

Penny recovered. "My brother has a fancy name too. Carlton James Chapman the third."

Toni's eyes widened, Sondra's got squinty. "Does he like it? Asked Toni "I dunno." Penny replied "We call him Skip."

"Skip Chapman hmm, not bad." said Toni, eyes rolling in thought.

How old is your brother? "asked the cold one

"Bout twelve" answered Penny with reserve.

"Really?" chimed Toni. "He like to fish or go on bike rides?"

Penny's eyes danced. "Sure and he has a real neat treehouse. You could come see it if you wanna."

"You bet." Answered Toni quickly, "but I can't now. I promised Dad I'd clean up the lakefront today. Just tell him I'll come by and see it someday. Which house is yours?"

Penny blushed. She didn't know her address. "Um it's white. And Daddy just painted the barn. Plus we have a driveway and Higby and Snuff."

"Is your name on the mailbox?" Toni asked patiently

"No." she answered sadly. "Just Daddy's."

Toni chuckled. "I'll find it Penny!"

Penny looked at Sondra, and said, "You could come too if you want to."

"What for?" she scoffed "I don't play in trees!" She glared at Toni, accusingly.

Penny blushed again. "I...I thought maybe you could play with me. There's lots to do in the barn and we cou..."

Sondra's laugh cut her off. "The barn? Really you expect me to play in a barn?" she mocked. "I'm sorry, I'm not seven; I'm nine going on ten and I am just way too busy to play like some girls my age do. Plus, I'm too mature anyway."

"Mature?" inquired Penny.

"Big for her britches." translated Toni dryly

"Oh," Penny sympathized, as though the child couldn't help it, "I hope you get better." Penny cocked her head and ventured, "What do you do for fun?"

Sondra smiled her first genuine smile and said, "Oh there are lots of things to do. I love shopping and parties and dance lessons, "she said dreamily.

"Don't forget the beauty shop." Toni interjected sarcastically.

Ignoring Toni, she continued, "Of course I'll really be busy now because I'm entering the Princess Pageant. Are you?"

"The whut?" asked Penny wide-eyed.

"The Princess Pageant. You know, they choose a winner out of a group of contestants and she gets crowned and reigns over the fair."

"Why does she do that?" Penny asked enthusiastically.

"Do what?"

"Rain on the fair?"

Sondra thought for a second and stuck her head out like a turtle. It ...ah...eh... oh never mind!"

Penny was embarrassed and afraid she would cry.

"For Pete's sake Sondra, she's only seven. How could she know about such things?" She hugged Penny's shoulders.

Not wanting to lose her audience, Sondra apologized grudgingly,"Oh I'm sorry. I meant the Princess takes part in all the festivities. She rides in the parade, things like that. It's like a beauty contest."

"Oh!" Penny smiled, "I hope you win."

Toni took a quick, shocked look at Penny.

Sondra was taken off guard, too, but recovered. "Oh I plan to, "then added, having won the upper hand,"I forgot you aren't old enough so none of this really matters. Come again sometime." she said without feeling as she walked away.

"Don't let her bother you Penny. She's not for real. Our Mother acts like that and Sunny just copies her."

Penny clapped her hand over her mouth in shock. "You called her Sunny!" she accused with muffled voice and eyes round like fried eggs.

"My Dad and I call her that just to be funny. I call my mother Ma too and she gets all huffy. They're both really freaky sometimes, you'll get used to it."

Penny's face contorted in her deep thoughts. "What's wrong Penny?"

Penny looked up at Toni, having been watching Sondra closely since Toni said "Sunny," right out loud, for fear she'd swoop down on them like an angry hawk. "Does Sondra ride the rides at the fair?"

"Never," stated Toni finally.

Penny shook her head. "I see what you mean 'bout freaky."

Toni laughed out loud and said, "I'm really glad you came over." She bent over and picked up her rake.

As Penny was leaving to return to her Aunt's house, they heard a voice from the deck of the big house. "Sondra, let's get started!"

Penny turned to watch.

Mrs. Burroughs continued. "We've got to get to the stores before everything get picked over. You know how people are."

Sondra turned briefly to smile at Penny who was giving her undivided attention. "Coming Mother. "she sang with exaggeration.

"Coming Mother." Toni mimicked "let's go shopping Mother, let's get more stuff Mother, and let's get snobbier Mother..." Toni stopped when she realized that Penny was still there gaping at her as she talked to herself. Toni burst out laughing at Penny's expression and Penny joined in.

CHAPTER XVII

Grumps

Skip dropped the suitcase he was carrying out to the car when Penny burst through the screen door behind him and bumped his back. "Holy cow Stupid! Dad's gonna hang me if his stuff is wrecked", he shouted. "Why don't you just get lost for a while?"

Skip rubbed at the dusty smudges on the black leather valise. Penny stood with her arms hanging limply beside her. "I didn't mean to do it Skip. I was running out to the tool shed for Daddy. He said to hurry." she cried.

"That's no excuse; you're not supposed to run in the house."

Penny stomped down the steps past her brother. "I'm telling Mommie you called me Stupid again!" she threatened, chin out and glaring.

Gramma came to the door "What's going on out here? Sounds like a chicken fight."

Skip told his grandmother how Penny had hit his back with the door causing him to drop the suitcase down the steps.

"But he called me Stupid, Gramma. Mommie said he's not allowed!" Penny's anger gave way to tears as she walked slowly toward the tool shed mumbling, "Everybody thinks I'm so dumb."

Skip dropped down on the steps. "Aw dang it, now I'm in trouble for making her cry."

Gramma sat down beside him and hugged his shoulder.

"I think everyone is a little touchy this morning Skip. Your Mom and Dad are grumpy too. Did you notice?"

"Yeah, I did, that's why I don't want to be in hot water now. Actually, I'm grumpy too," he mused,"Don't know why."

"Well Honey, your Dad is leaving for Lincoln today. His vacation is over. That's kind of depressing, don't you think?"

Skip protested, "But he's done the same thing for three years now Gramma."

"I know that," she replied, "but the same kinds of things happened last year. Remember how Penny spilled the basket of blueberries all over the kitchen and your mom locked herself in the den for an hour?"

Skip laughed. "Hey you're right, Dad got ticked at Mom and Penny blamed it on me because she said my ball glove was in her way."

Gramma nodded. "So there you are same circumstances, different year." She patted his arm. "Let's try to turn things around so everyone can help Dad enjoy his last vacation day."

Penny approached the porch still scowling at Skip. Skip stood up. "I'm sorry Penny, I'm just grumpy; Course it was an accident."

He opened the door for Penny who brightened. "Me too Skip."

Gramma followed Penny into the house. "That's more like it, besides sillies, he'll be back Friday night."

"That's a long time Gramma!" pouted Penny. "I wish he could stay here the whole summer with us."

"Wouldn't that be nice," agreed Gramma as she ushered Penny through the kitchen toward the den. "Best get that box of hinges to your Dad. He wants to be sure he takes them with him. He plans to get them plated this week."

Penny looked down at the boot box full of hinges, knobs and latches. "I think they're pretty just the way they are."

"Wait 'til you see them next week Pen, they'll look brand new." Skip added as he finished wiping down the suitcase with a damp cloth and headed for the door.

Lunchtime was pleasant thanks to Gramma's counseling. Another reason there had been some tension was the nagging, but not convincing thought, in the back of Jim's, mind about the incident at the school and Stan. After all, here he was leaving him in the house with his wife and children. But Carl Sr., a very good judge of character, was able to persuade them to continue to believe in Stan's innocence. "He simply doesn't act as though he has anything to hide;" he told them "He could have taken off long ago, and without a trace. After all" he reasoned, "he knows he's a suspect like lots of other people. And remember, the investigators questioned him at length and if his alibis didn't check out, they'd have let us know."

"I really think you're right Dad," Jim agreed. "He offered to move out when I leave because it might rest my mind about going. Shirley about had a fit. And another thing I noticed is that he doesn't seem to mind the questions. In fact, he brings the robbery up once in a while, himself, if he's been to Barlow and hears something new." Jim snapped his suitcase. "I felt kind of bad the other night though when I mentioned casually about him waxing the floors, and the Ag room being concrete. He just laughed and said he would think anyone would know you wouldn't mix paint or fill hot waxing machines on the tile floors."

Shirley tore the to-do list off the tablet she had been writing on and followed the men out to the kitchen. "Well, my biggest worry about Stan is that he will leave us. He's been so much help and it would be really good to have all those other jobs done around here that he's planning to do."

"You're telling me!" Jim agreed, "It would take all my weekend time to get even half those things done. I can't believe how much work there is to do around here." Then Jim recalled something.

"That reminds me Dad, could you get my chain saw sharpened? Stan said he'd cut up those fallen trees down by the pond."

"No problem," Carl assured him, "mine needs sharpened too. We've cleared away nearly everyone's storm damage around the lake except mine and Frank's. They had a backlog of sharpening last time I was in, so I was figuring on getting the saw in this week and getting cutting that done. Actually, I 'spect Stan and I'll work together." He laughed. "Sounds like Stan would be too busy to go to jail even if he did commit the robbery."

"Well that's an injustice if I ever heard one! I'm too busy, but I have to go to work!" Jim whined.

"Aww," Shirley and Gramps teased at the same time.

"Sorry Son "said Carl "you're the boss. It's not our fault you can't pencil in a few more days off."

Jim nodded, "I know. I plan to every year and then don't think of it until I have to go back to Lincoln without the family. Besides, I like the holidays off, before the big rush, at the end of the year."

Penny met the trio at the doorway. "Here's your stuff Daddy, "she said brightly.

"Good," he said as he took the box. "Didn't drop any did you?"

"No!" Penny responded tartly. "I'm not stupid" she added convincingly. Jim smiled at his plucky little daughter. "You're anything but stupid, One Cent. Silly, maybe, but defiantly not stupid."

"Yeah" she giggled as he pinched her cheek. "Silly."

Jim left right after lunch for the two hour drive to the city armed with instructions about newspaper delivery and directions for operating the new dishwasher. He also had a grocery list which Shirley had remarked to Jim's mom, would probably be ignored.

"Jim's a compulsive shopper. He'll find out the hard way, like always," she laughed as she tried to imagine his first few days alone.

After an easy trip into Lincoln, Jim ran errands and spent the remainder of the weekend cutting grass and visiting neighbors. Late Sunday night, over overcooked hamburgers, he thought, "Tomorrow after work I'll drive down to Andy Russo's and gets these things restored." The box of hardware sat on the kitchen table where it had been since he arrived the two days before. He fondled a drawer pull and tried to imagine a big blue ribbon hanging on the front of the chiffierobe at the fair. He broke into a grin. "Can't wait," he said aloud in the big quiet house.

CHAPTER XVIII

New Interests

After her father left Penny took Snuff and went to her room. "I don't like it when Daddy leaves, "she moaned to her fuzzy friend. She flopped on the bed and began leafing idly through the Barlow Festival booklet that had come the week before. Her eyes focused on an adorable puppy whose picture filled half a page in the book. Below the picture she read

> Barlow Festival Pet Show
> Opening Day
>
> Largest, Smallest, Funniest, Prettiest
> All domestic pets

"All dom...hmm." She stuck on the word domestic. Intrigued, she jumped off her bed to go find someone to help her read the unfamiliar word. Penny thought as she glanced at the article, "I could be in the pet show with Snuff. Bet I could win a prize too. Then that smartie Sondra would be nice to me. "She turned to announce her plans to Snuff but the alert cat was already down to the kitchen, anticipating a treat.

Skip was untangling a pile of rope when he heard bicycle brakes squeak behind him. He looked up at the unknown girl who was propping her bike against the barn. Standing up, with the ropes in both hands, Skip smiled shyly. "Hi."

"Hi," she returned softly, "I'm Toni Burroughs. Your sister invited me up to see your treehouse." Then she blushed. "That is if you're Skip Chapman."

Skip smiled broadly. "Yeah, I'm Skip. Penny told me about you and your family moving in next to my aunt and uncle. C'mon, I'll show you around. I was just getting this rigging ready to haul out there."

"Pulleys?" Toni inquired.

"Yeah, my dad gave them to me but he didn't have time to help me with them. I have a pretty good idea how to do them but...," he faded and looked at the mess.

"Oh please, let me help you. Our table did four different systems for a science project last year. I'm not sure I'll remember everything but I really think I could help you."

Skip sighed, "I'm sure you could. It's a job for two people. My Dad's out of town, my Gramps is setting up a booth for the Senior Center and Stan is at the fairgrounds unloading trucks. That leaves Penny or my Mom." He shook his head. "Not good choices."

"Well then let's get started!" Toni suggested enthusiastically as she picked up the remaining ropes to the well used block and tackle sets.

They walked side by side toward the orchard.

Think she's a little taller than me Skip thought as he straightened up his shoulders.

"You going into sixth grade Toni?"

Toni shook her head. "Nope, seventh. Junior High School." She looked at Skip. "Wish I wasn't. I'm not ready for all of that stuff."

Skip looked at her puzzled.

"Oh, it'll be okay, I mean I can do the work and all, I just don't think I'm ready to give up being a kid, you know. My Mom is planning to put me in a snob club. Dress me up like a model and... ugh! I get sick thinking about it."

"Yeah," Skip agreed sympathetically.

Toni laughed at Skip, making a face in disgust. "How about you?"

Skip blushed, "I'm just in middle school this fall. Sixth grade. My birthday isn't 'til November. I'll be twelve then." They stopped under an apple tree, to catch their breath.

Toni picked up the conversation. "I just turned in June. I'm one of the youngest in my class that I know of. She caught a glimpse of the treehouse. Ready."

They hoisted the heavy equipment on their shoulders and completed the walk. When they reached the treehouse, Skip looked hopefully at Toni.

Toni stood looking up and smiled what Skip assessed, as a very pretty smile.

"This is awesome Skip! I've never seen one this nice before, or as big."

Skip grinned sheepishly. "I think it turned out pretty nice myself. Let's go up. You haven't seen anything yet."

Toni stepped to the ladder and climbed up without hesitation, calling over her shoulder, "I wish I had a place like this to go. A place where I could be alone and think."

Skip was astounded. "That's why I built it and why I named it THE HIDEAWAY."

As they stood on the platform and looked around at the farmlands, Toni reflected, "You are sure nice to let me come up here Skip. I know this is a really special place for you. It's fantastic!"

Skip really blushed this time and felt he should say something but didn't want to sound corny or like a little kid. Finally he just said, "Thanks Toni," with a sincere oversized smile, on his face.

A while after Toni and Skip set to work, straightening out all the rope and measuring it, Penny came out to tell Skip about the pet show and Snuff. Toni and Skip were deeply engrossed, rigging the pulley system.

"Toni! You came!" called the bumpy voice and they looked up from their project to see Penny running across the uneven orchard.

"Hi Penny," they said in duet, Toni smiling broadly.

Penny ran up to Toni and hugged her waist. "See Skip's treehouse?"

"See it? I sure did, and it's honestly the most wonderful treehouse I have ever seen."

Skip drank up the compliment as he began picking up the ropes and pulleys. "These will really make the treehouse classy. Toni and I are going to hang them tomorrow," He said not even trying to conceal his excitement.

Penny held up the booklet and said with an air of importance all her own. "Well I have to go to Barlow tomorrow, on business."

"On business?" Skip responded amused.

"Yup," she said proudly. "Gonna sign Snuff up in the pet show." She handed the booklet to Toni who was joined by Skip.

"Really? Think she'll win anything? "Toni wondered aloud.

"Yeah," chorused Skip. She's just a house cat."

"Nuh uh!" Penny said. Mommie said she's a…um…. can I see that a minute? She reached for the booklet. "She's a …" Penny scrolled the page slowly with her finger…..domexixs! Isn't that lucky?"

Skip nodded amused. "Domestic, Penny…that's right, she is. I forgot," he added generously.

"Plus!" she shouted excitedly, "We hafta sign up Daddy."

"For the pet show?" Toni teased.

Penny laughed merrily at Toni. "No, for the chifferboard contest."

Toni looked at Skip. "Shuffleboard?" she asked quietly as he chuckled and waved her off.

"I'll tell you all about it tomorrow. It's quite a story." He looked back at Penny in hopes of sending her on her way.

'I'm getting soooo excited 'bout the fair!" Penny sang.

Toni let out a huge, attention-worthy sigh. "You wouldn't say that if you had to live at my house." She walked over to the ropes and began pulling them toward the ladder roughly. "I'll be excited, once that stupid Princess Pageant is over!" She looked at her new friends and explained, as if to apologize for her attitude. "Sondra is so overbearing that we hardly ever hear about anything else. She and my mother talk about it constantly. Me and Dad might as well not exist. He leaves in a huff and stays away most of the time." Her mind wandered away as she coiled rope. Eventually, after about a minute, she smiled a melancholy smile and finished hauling with Skip and brushed off her clothes. "I need to get home now." She announced, her happy mood destroyed.

"Sure," said Skip, partly out of relief. "Man Toni," Skip said appreciatively, "thanks for your help. I'd probably still be untangling rope. We'll walk you back to your bike," Skip offered, including Penny in the gesture.

They made plans to meet at the treehouse early the next morning and listened to Penny ramble on about the pet show as they walked through the orchard.

Toni jumped on her bike and rode down the driveway. "Bye Skip, bye Penny, I had a great time."

"Isn't she nice Skip?" Penny smiled as she waved.

"She's real neat Pen," he said as he pulled the barn door shut. Just about the neatest girl I've ever met. She not all giggly and stuff."

Penny waved the booklet at the small figure out on the road and sang, "Skip's got a girl-friend.!"

Skip thought about taking after her but just shrugged instead. "Who knows? C'mon, let's see what's for dinner. "Think we'll eat lunch in the tree house tomorrow," he thought out loud.

"Oh goody!" Penny screeched.

"Not you silly, me and Toni."

"Phooey" blasted Penny as she stomped toward the house.

Hoping to avoid any Toni discussion at the supper table, he reminded Penny, "You won't be home tomorrow, anyway, remember."

CHAPTER XIX

Registration

It's a good thing Stan had advised that Shirley and Penny get an early start because the lines were forming long before the ten o'clock opening of registration day at the Barlow Fairgrounds.

Registering Snuff in the pet show took quite a while because there were so many children and a few owners brought their pets with them also. Penny wanted to bring Snuff but was told it wasn't necessary, and it would be hard on Snuff. Penny thoroughly enjoyed the chaos and was content to watch people try to handle their kids and animals while they waited and signed forms. After Shirley filled out the entry form they were invited to go look at the facility where the animals would be for the judging.

"I think Snuff's gonna be mad at me Mommie." Penny worried as she looked at the cages that the pets were required to be in when their handlers were not showing them.

Shirley surveyed the building. "Well, she'll settle down after a while, I'm sure. The cages are nice and big and the building is airy. Don't you remember all the animals last year? They seemed to enjoy all the attention. I'm sure she'll be fine for part of a day," she assured Penny who had clouded over considerably.

Entering Jim's chiffierobe didn't take long at all, so Penny and her mother had time to walk around the busy grounds and checked out the pavilion that was reserved every year for the family reunion. All around them they could hear crews hammering and sawing as they repaired buildings and erected booths on the midway.

Penny watched a group, from a summer park program, building a puppet theater while she waited at a picnic table for her mother to bring their lunch from the concession hall.

Just as they settled in to eat their lunch, Penny looked up to see Sondra and her mother approaching the picnic area. Shirley recognized Mrs. Burroughs and invited her to join them. Mrs. Burroughs, as she apparently preferred to be called, as she had never said otherwise, and Shirley looked over the pageant rules. Penny and Sondra sat eating and talking at the other end of the table.

"I hate eating outside!" whined Sondra. "There are way too many bugs!"

Penny looked at Sondra and realized that Sondra was really very uncomfortable with the few flies that were around the table.

"What will you do 'bout them when you're in the contest?" Penny asked flipping a french-fry at her mouth.

Sondra spoke confidently, "I'm sure they'll have a nice place for the contestants Penny. When my cousin Larae was in a pageant in Winnetka, they had a gazebo and an air conditioned trailer."

"Really?" said Penny impressed. "That would be nice." She smiled at Sondra and then twisted her face. Blushing, she asked, "What's a gazebo?"

Sondra managed a warming smile at the elfish face. "A gazebo is a pretty little yard house that's open all around, but it's cool and shady. The one in Winnetka had screen on it, so there were no bugs!" Sondra's eyes were big to emphasize "bugs" and she and Penny laughed.

Right about then Mrs. Burroughs spoke, "Sondra, we mustn't be late for our appointments. We've so much to do before the pageant. I'm not sure how we'll manage."

Sondra's expression changed, and Penny couldn't read it, but she did know that Sondra had been smiling and now she wasn't. "Yes, I know that Mother." They got up and left after a quick good bye.

Penny got off the bench and grabbed her french-fries; half eaten hot dog and pop. She climbed on the seat beside her Mother, sloshing her pop. "Sondra was really nice to me today Mommie. She's so pretty," she added dreamily.

"She certainly is Penny and do you know what?"

Penny tilted her head.

"I think that you are good for her. I think her mother is forgetting she is just a little girl."

Penny hugged her mother's arm. "You never forget I'm a little girl, do you Mommie?"

Shirley laughed and shook her head as she blotted pop off Penny's shorts. "How could I?"

CHAPTER XX

Small World

The air was hot and muggy when Jim drove down to the east side of town. He had come to the plating company a number of times before to have hardware plated, or to visit his pal Andy. Jim was always interested in all the changes in the growing industrial area. Andy Russo, owner of Russo Plating greeted Jim at the office door.

"Looks like things are picking up around here Andy," Jim said as they shook hands.

The men left the office through the rear entrance, Andy in the lead. "They are," he smiled enthusiastically. "We just bought the building directly across from this plant and that one on the end past the yards. Fact is, we'd own this whole side of the park, but the realtor leased the building next to our shop to some outfit from Missouri, before I could even knew it was available. We're running a good bit of time-and-a-half production, and we may go back to two full shifts by the first of the year. Lester and three others have been working an extra shift with me the last few nights."

"I've had a big year too," Jim offered. "I'd have loved to have taken a couple more weeks off this summer but I'll never have things ready for quarterlies if I'm sitting in a boat out on the lake!"

The men entered a large building where a couple of workers were tending to vats of shimmery liquids and racks of parts. They continued on to a smaller area and were met by Andy's oldest employee, Lester. "Hey Jim" he greeted. Whatcha got this time?"

Jim handed the box to him. "Hardware from a nice maple piece I refinished. How are you doing Lester?"

Lester examined the pulls, handles and latches. "Good Jim can't really complain. Work too hard, taxes are up, wife left me but the Cubbies are winning." The trio laughed and joked as Lester put the pieces on a mesh screen, bathed them in a cleaning solution, and then rolled the tray on a cart to the plating vat. Lester checked each piece over carefully as he lifted them with tongs and placed them onto a small conveyor that took them through a dryer.

"This is the fun part, "Jim gushed, as he shifted nervously, while Lester worked with his treasurers. Lester pushed a button that removed a stainless steel lid from a vat, and the conveyor moved slowly over the vat. The conveyor separated when Lester slid a bolt up and a golden mesh tray received the pieces as the conveyor gently dropped them as it separated. Lester fastened each side of the tray with a hasp and then lowered the tray down into the shiny metallic solution, using a lever. He checked a gauge or two and turned toward Jim smiling.

"You're allowed to breathe Jim, "he said laughing. When Lester brought up the tray, the three men beamed their approval.

"I knew they would turn out beautiful." Jim said enthusiastically.

"Nice Lester, finish 'em up and pack 'em to go okay?" Andy directed." Jim and I are going to get some supper."

As they were pulling out of the parking lot in Andy's car, Jim looked over the resurrected industrial park. He craned his neck to look through Andy's side window.

"That looks like one of Roy or Ron Donaldson's trucks parked over there at that new outfit's place. Their trucking company is out past our place.

Andy squinted against the lowering sun and leaned into the window. "Yep. Donaldson's Transfer, Brownsville," he read.

Jim shook his head. "Small world," he said as he turned back and watched traffic. "Maybe they expanded," he surmised.

"Steakhouse?" Andy inquired

"You had to ask?" Jim's replied, sarcastically.

Out at the farm, Penny and her mother were fussing over Snuff, guided by a booklet they had bought on grooming and showing cats. Snuff wasn't very enthused about being brushed and even less so about getting her ears cleaned.

"Boy Mommie, Snuff's wors'en me," Penny complained.

Shirley dried her hands. "Well she didn't do too badly but I think we'll wait right before the morning of the pet show to try this again."

"Yeah," agreed Penny, She's already mad enough. Look at her look at me. I don't even think she wants to *be* in the pet show."

Mrs. Chapman studied Penny and Snuff. "I really don't think she is thinking about that Penny but if it's going to upset you we can always withdraw her."

Penny's eyes opened wide. "Oh no! I don't want to do that. I want her in it. She put her face down close to Snuff's and spoke baby talk to her. "That smartie Sondra isn't the only one doing something special at the fair, is she?" She shot a look at her mother. I want Snuff to win a blue ribbon. "Penny stroked the cat as she spoke earnestly.

"Oh, so that's it "said her mother. "No wonder you're feeling Iffy about this Penny, you're using Snuff to try to show up Sondra."

Penny failed to look at her Mother. "Nah uh, I'm not, huh Snuff?" she cooed as she scooped her up and walked out of the den.

CHAPTER XXI

Perch!

"Got a bite!" shouted Skip, "he's on good." Toni dropped her pole and hurried toward Skip on the opposite end of the dock. They looked into the water in search of the fish that was pulling Skip's line back and forth.

"Oooh! I see him Skip, he's a beauty. "Skip shifted his feet and followed the lead.

"Yeah! I see him too. Perch."

"Naw," Toni scoffed "Too big, that's a little pike. Betcha."

Skip took a quick skeptical look at Toni then turned his attention to the fighting fish. "On a dough ball?" he gasped between coaxing the fish. "C'mon in baby, give it up!"

"Makes no difference," Toni came back as she reached the net down to the water.

"Fights like a gutsy little perch," he argued. "Atta boy, c'mon in."

Toni dropped to her knees and scooped at the water guided by the fish line. "He's tangled in the dock post, Skip!" Toni reached out and tried to move the line around and free him.

"Drat it! He's really stuck." Skip shouted. He tugged gently once more and the line broke away causing him to step back.

Toni spotted the fish and made a last effort lunge with the net. "It's no use Skip, he got away." Toni searched the water and dropped her head.

Skip put down his pole and leaned over and tapped Toni. She looked up at his big smile. He offered her his hand and helped her to her feet with both hands. Speaking softly, almost a whisper, Skip said, "It's okay Toni." He paused, and then added, "Perch are smart!"

Toni's eyes widened and her nostrils flared. "Skip Chapman, you saw him. You know I'm right. It was a pike!" She freed her hands and pushed Skip soundly on the chest and laughed as he splashed into the lake.

Skip came up sputtering and laughing and then a devious look came across his face as he heaved himself up on the side dock, trapping Toni.

"No Skip!" she begged as she backed closer to the end of the dock.

"I...I...didn't mean it. *You* were right!" she blubbered. "Imagine that, a tough little perch...Skip!"

Skip stood right in front of Toni. "So!" he bellowed. "see it my way now do ya? Think I'll show mercy heh?" he grinned.

"We could talk about it" she said weakly trying to sound frightened.

"Ha!" he yelled as he pushed her off the dock at the deep end. As she was going under, Skip heard her call out, "Pike! ...bbbbbbbb."

Skip stood laughing at the beach when Toni came wading in. Her progress was hindered by her convulsive laughter.

Skip spun around when he heard a second laugh, not at all like Toni's. "Hi Sondra, "he greeted, encouraged by her smile. "Going swimming?"

"Oh no!" Sondra said quickly "I was just watching you guys. Looks like fun though."

Skip's smile faded as he studied Sondra. "Yeah, we always have fun. Why don't you put on some grunge sometime and join us?" he coaxed.

"Yeouch!" yelped Skip when Toni snapped him lightly with her wet towel. He grabbed the towel and pointed to the lake. "Ready for round two?"

"No, you win." Toni laughed. "Hi Sunny, what's up?"

Sondra shrugged "Oh nothing, I was just..." Sondra stopped talking when a car horn sounded. "Gotta go!" she said, starting up the hill.

Skip and Toni watched her walk up the steps and waved to Mrs. Burroughs.

"You know what I think?" Skip asked as they gathered up their fishing and swimming gear. "I sorta think Sondra would rather be playing than chasing all over town with your mother and all her stuffy friends."

Toni nodded in agreement. "I know what you mean, I've thought that a thousand times. But I also wonder sometimes if she could ever even act like a normal kid. It's like she's ruined."

They walked toward the bathhouse next to the three bay marina on the Burroughs lakefront. "I doubt if we'll ever find out Skip. Mother is having so much fun with her little monster, that I guarantee you, she'll never give her up. I feel bad for Sondra. I really do, but honestly, I'm just glad it's not me!"

Skip's eyes widened "Boy I'll say! Can't picture me pushing someone with Sondra's temperament in the lake!"

Toni waved the remark off. "Don't worry Skip. Sondra wouldn't have argued with you." She slipped quickly into the shower room and locked the door.

Skip shrugged his shoulders and turned to walk away. Still in earshot, he heard Toni laugh.

"What's so funny?" he asked the locked door.

"I was just thinking, that's all," she called out laughing.

"What?" he persisted.

"I was thinking about Sondra. About how she doesn't know *anything* about fish" she paused, "either!"

She turned on the shower and steam rolled out the vents at Skip who stood staring at the door. He growled.

"What's that? Can't hear you! Shower's on." she laughed.

Skip walked away vowing to himself to find a way to get even tomorrow.

CHAPTER XXII

No Kidding!

Stan and Carl Sr. were congratulating themselves on all their accomplishments of the week as Carl pulled into the hardware parking lot at the crossroads south of the lake. The men climbed out of the truck joking about what to do with any free time, if it ever happened. Both men pulled chainsaws out of the bed of the truck.

"Hope they can get right to these. I'd like to get Jim's trees cut up by day after tomorrow and spend a couple of days hauling in the wood for the holidays," said Carl.

"You know sir, when we start clearing those trees at Jim's we'll be disturbing a couple of lovebirds in the orchard."

"Really?" sympathized Carl, until he saw the twinkle in Stan's eyes.

"Oh, lovebirds. You think they're girlfriend-boyfriend like that?" Carl probed.

"Naw," laughed Stan. "Not really. I think they just enjoy being together. Neither one acts like it's a romancy kind of thing. Fact is, Skip said he just thinks she cool. I just like to tease them."

"Skipper's not ready. I guarantee that," said Carl as he thought back. "He's his Dad all over. Jim never saw it coming when he and Shirley started out. They'd grown up together, and did the dating and prom like everyone, always as a couple. But Jim left for college before he realized what she meant to him. Hope Skip's equally as slow to commit".

Stan held the door for Carl. "Or, he could be like me, thirty five and still drifting."

Carl laughed over his shoulder, "That's a little extreme Pal."

Inside the store the men headed for the back where the chainsaws would be sharpened. While Carl gave the clerk some information, Stan went searching for work gloves.

Stan was turning away from the counter after paying for his gloves, when he heard a voice from somewhere behind him call, "Hey Southworthless!"

He turned and spotted a stocky, red-headed man coming toward him. Grinning, Stan greeted the man with a handshake and bear hug. "Leo, I thought maybe you left the country. How are you?"

"Pretty fair, Leo answered, laughing. How about yourself?"

"Just fine. Busy all the time. I'm working out at Jim Chapman's. He paused to let it sink in and added for clarification, "Frank Chapman, from the mill?" asking with his eyebrows, to help Leo associate. "You know, it's his brother, Jim. They have the farmhouse after highway 6 crosses Lake Road.

"Oh, okay. Been out there all along?" Leo asked.

"Oh yeah, the timing was good. Jim was eating away his vacation painting the barn. Hired me on the spot." Stan knitted his brows, "So where have you been? No one I've talked to has seen you, since our last job."

"Oh I've been right here, over at Donaldson's."

"Since the school job?"

"Yeah... I... uh..." Leo was saying, when he noted Carl approaching them. Stan reached for Carl's arm to bring him into the group and said, "Leo, I'd like for you to meet Mr. Chapman, Jim's Dad. "He looked fondly at Leo, and continued, "My old carnie pal Leo Sweeny."

"Hello Leo. Your reputation has preceded you," Carl joked as they shook hands. The three men worked their way out of the store and stood on the wooden porch exchanging small talk. After a few minutes, Stan's curiosity got to him and he changed the subject. "Leo, how come none of us ran in to you at the sheriff's office? They let you off already?"

Leo mocked being offended. "What are you talking about Stan, I haven't been in trouble since Porky and I got caught up in that little brawl at Dunn County and you hadda post bail." Leo said as he rolled his eyes.

"Yeah, I remember that," Stan acknowledged, "but the Sheriff said they were calling in everybody who worked at the school this summer."

"For what?" Leo asked half amused.

Stan and Carl exchanged puzzled glances. They turned toward Leo, who was equally puzzled and beginning to think he was missing something important.

Carl looked at Leo seriously." Leo, do you know that the school had a big robbery?"

"No! When?" Leo asked, intrigued Stan threw up his hands, walked a half circle and said, "Right after we worked there Leo! After we did the painting and floors."

Leo tossed his head back. "You're kidding! What's to steal?"

Stan's eyes widened. "Somebody stole the equipment that was in the old shop...all those big crates!"

Leo's eyes narrowed as he held up his hands. "Wait a sec... hold it right there Sherlock," he said, shaking his head in Stan's face. "That stuff wasn't stolen. It was just the wrong shipment. The Principal, what's his name...Osborne, knows that, why didn't somebody ask him?"

Stan was speechless.

"What makes you say that Leo? Who told you it was the wrong shipment?" Carl asked calmly.

Leo looked at Mr. Chapman and Stan in a new light. He ran the past few weeks through his mind and figured out where to begin.

"Uh, well...I'm working for the Donaldsons." He tipped his head to the left and the two men looked across the crossroads at the Donaldson's trucking business. "I went to work for them right after we did the school job" he continued. Looking at Stan, "If you remember Buddy; us guys on the painting crew finished up before you guys doing floors. Ron hired me even me before I was done at the school." He looked at Carl, and explained. "I'm good at doing tires, any kind, any size. I noticed they had a flat on their truck when they delivered the boiler and heaters. I helped with the compressor and we got it changed real quick. Ron liked my work, and so the rest is history."

Carl nodded, "How does that figure in? You working for them, I mean."

Leo continued. "Well, somebody hired out a couple trucks and a forklift, and we worked several hours, at the school, almost all night, loading."

"Night?" Carl asked curiously.

"Yeah, the trucks came in about eight thirty. We had closed up at the garage and I just finished eating and was watching TV. Ron came back and said he needed me to help at the school. Rush job." Leo scratched his head. I don't really see what the problem is." He looked at Stan. "They think you swiped the equipment?" He looked into their eyes back and forth twice. "Or that we did it?"

Carl and Stan were on the same thought. Something was wrong with this story and Leo was in the middle, whether he realized it or not. They communicated nonverbally.

"Leo, you had better come with us," Carl said seriously, I'll buy you guys lunch at the Lakeside and we can talk."

"About what?" Leo said defensively.

Stan put his arm around the shoulder of his red faced friend and said, "Leo, some things need answers. You're going to have to go to the sheriff."

"But I didn't do anything!" Man Stan, you're spooking me." He protested, "There is a logical explanation to this and believe me, I'm innocent of any wrongdoing. Why should I go to the sheriff? Let Ron or Roy. "He looked at Carl as they approached the truck. Carl met his gaze. "Aw man,!" he moaned, knowing there was no use in arguing.

CHAPTER XXIII

In the Dark

Settled in a secluded corner of the restaurant, the trio began to piece the story from Leo's point of view. Leo's time, the past few weeks, had been spent working or in the back of the truck garage in two tiny rooms. He spent long days doing truck maintenance and was responsible for the custodial work in the bays, restroom and his living area. He ate in the kitchen of Lil's Diner next to the garage, also owned by the Donaldson's.

"I never went anywhere. Some days I didn't see anyone but Lil and Ron Donaldson." He paused, stirring his coffee. "They never mentioned anything about it, and now, I'm thinking that maybe there's a reason," Leo worried. "Fact is, I wouldn't have even run into you two if I hadn't needed a flashlight bulb. One of the guys usually get s me everything I need, but they are both out of town. "He brightened as he said, "So I gave myself a couple of hours off."

"Didn't you ever talk to anyone?" Stan questioned. "Drivers?"
"Never heard nothing" Leo responded.

Carl shook his head and wondered aloud. "What about the papers and the news on TV? How did you miss those?"

Leo blushed. "Never took to reading much," he said simply and deferred to Stan.

"It's true" Stan said softly. "We've always helped him."

"Yeah, and the TV I have doesn't work very well, but I don't look at the news anyhow." He reflected. "Too depressing and it's 'bout people and places I don't know. Mostly, I just watch fishing shows and old movies." Smiling, he glanced again at Stan.

"This guy!" Stan said affectionately. "When we get a room together at a motel between fairs, he's a nut with the TV. One time, I'll never forget..."

Leo lowered his head to hide his smile.

Stan continued, "He found a John Wayne marathon on one station and a bass fishing weekend on another station."

Carl laughed, and said, "S'pose that means you had to find your own entertainment, right?"

Stan and Leo laughed. Stan confirmed Carl's remark, saying, "I left after two hours and went bowling with the other fellas we work with, and when I got back at around three hours later, Leo was still watching TV!"

Carl shook his head knowingly, and remarked, "Sounds like Jim and an antique show weekend." Then he recalled Leo's predicament.

"So, tell me Leo, where did you guys take the equipment?"

Leo took a deep breath, having forgotten where the conversation was headed. "Got me. Ron and Roy went with it. They were gone overnight. Ron came back to the garage the next day for a while, seems to me. Don't know where Roy was. He's really not around all that much. Two or three times a week, usually. Leo nodded his head as he recalled. "All I know is I had to work late that day 'cause there wasn't anybody else around. But...that's not suspicious. Sometimes it's busy and more often, it's quiet when all the trucks are jobbed out."

Stan shook his head. "Surprised you stayed with that job. You're such a free spirit and social butterfly."

Leo nodded in agreement. 'That's true enough, but the money's great. His eyes lit up as he continued, "Roy even offered me a permanent job. Working on the fleet."

Stan was interested. "Going to take it?"

Leo laughed and his eyes danced when he said, "Heck no! I don't want to stay in one place, 'specially not in Lincoln. That's where I'd work. I think that's why they gave me the raise, to get me to sign on. "Leo smiled mischievously. "So I haven't told him I wasn't taking it yet" he chuckled. Are you going back with us on the circuit?" Stan asked hopefully.

The men began eating as soon as the food hit the table.

"Sure am," Leo said cheerfully. Ron signed me up on the work roster last week. I told them I had to work Barlow. Told them you was counting on me."

Stan disagreed between bites. "No he didn't. I checked it yesterday. Everybody else has signed. That's why I figured you left town."

Leo's face turned beet red. "He said he signed me up, said I was working grandstands and night watch! That's what I requested."

Stan shook his head and said, "afraid not Leo. I haven't given assignments yet. That's tomorrow night." Stan sat waiting for Leo's next question.

Leo was speechless.

Carl heaved a sigh saying, "Well guys, let's finish our coffee and then head for Barlow. I'm a little concerned about the Donaldson's showing up. They're gonna know something's up, Leo not being there. If they had anything to do with this crime, they aren't going to let Leo out of their sight. And come fair time, they obviously had plans to have Leo in Lincoln, or at least away from here… permanently." The three men looked at each other, considering Carl's remark.

"What do we do now?" asked Leo. I might be in over my head here and I don't know anyone around that could help me.

I'm just a roving laborer and I guarantee, that'll go against me. Always does."

Stan agreed with Leo, even though he didn't voice it.

Carl held up his hand to protest. "Hold it there, there's lots of good folks around here that will hear your story."

They got up and Carl ushered them out. "Clearly, Leo, you need to go to the sheriff. We'll take you over to get your things if the brothers aren't there. Then we'll head for Barlow."

Stan spoke for the first time in several minutes. "Shirley, your wife and the kids are at the fairgrounds cleaning the pavilion, Mr. Chapman".

"That's right," commented Carl. "That's right. Then let's run by and let them know about the change in plans and see what they think about all of this." He looked at Leo and explained. "They were at the school when the theft was discovered."

Carl clapped Leo's shoulder and suggested, "My son Jim has lots of legal friends in Lincoln. I'll call him and if it turns out that you need a lawyer, we'll get you one."

Leo dropped his head, "Thanks a lot, Mr. Chapman" he said weakly.

Stan wore a sympathetic expression. "Thanks Carl thanks a lot."

CHAPTER XXIV

New View

When Jim pulled into the driveway on Friday night, he was surprised to see that the house was dark and Higby was tied up. "Nobody's home," he mumbled, disappointed. "Wonder what's going on." He knew that it was out of the ordinary for his family not to be there to welcome him back at the end of his work week. As he went up the steps, he searched for the farmhouse key and dropped his bags to hasten entry when he heard the telephone ringing.

"Hello," he answered breathless and then smiled. "Yep, I was just coming in. Where is everybody?" Jim listened as his wife gave him a sketchy account of the events of the day. He scribbled notes on the notepad and asked Shirley to spell Leo's last name. His eyes widened and his mouth dropped open. "Wow! Listen Shirley, of course I don't mind if Leo stays with us. I think the sheriff's right. He shouldn't go back out to Donaldson's. You, Mom and the kids can come on out home. And Shirley, tell Dad I'm going to make some quick phone calls and then I'll drive over to the sheriff's office and meet them."

Jim hung up and went to retrieve his briefcase containing his pocket directory. "Um, Friday night," he muttered. "Sure hope I can find Bill or someone from his office."

The Chapman farmhouse was buzzing with activity Saturday morning as everyone made final preparations for the fair. Shirley and Wilma were busy cooking for the reunion as well as for the brood at the house for the day. Jim, Carl, Leo and Bill Whitlock, Jim's friend from the DA's office in Lincoln, were mostly trying to keep out of the way. Stan had gone to work at the fairgrounds. Leo wanted to go, seeking security in being with his pals, but reluctantly agreed to stay behind.

On a long shot, Jim had mentioned the Donaldson's truck parked by Russo's Plating and they were awaiting word on that. Andy Russo had turned his office over to Lincoln investigators and they were petitioning for a search warrant for the building next door. The phone rang so frequently for Bill that everyone eventually stopped waiting with baited breath every time a call came through. Bill, who was genuinely happy to be visiting the Chapman's took the events in stride, treating it as just another day "at the office".

Bill had tried to reassure Leo that things would work out. Leo was nearly in shock from the past twenty four hours activity and he was beginning to think that he had been a patsy and it upset him, first to think that he'd been pulled in and secondly because he really liked the Donaldsons. Unfortunately, everything they pieced together so far pointed to the Donaldson's involvement.

"Relax Leo. I can just about guarantee that your life will be back to normal by this time tomorrow," Bill said, confidently.

Leo had disagreed, at one point, earlier. "No sir, I don't think so. I really doubt if anything will be normal again. You don't know how hard it is for fair workers. Some one of us's always getting picked up. I got a friend doing time, never done a thing wrong. Deputy Sheriff had a robbery to pin on someone. Louse was running in the primary and he and his party framed my buddy" he said sadly.

The men listened thoughtfully. Stan nodded his head when Bill assured Leo, but that was for Leo's benefit because his gut instinct was the same as Leo's, and it made his stomach queasy.

Toni and Sondra had come up to visit the farm and the four kids decided to go out to the treehouse to get away from all the commotion. Penny pled their case and managed to collect a picnic lunch from Wilma, who was in charge of the kitchen while Shirley dug baskets and linens out of the closet. Penny rationalized, "To keep us outta your feet Gramma."

It had taken Toni a long time to persuade Sondra to come with her and it also took all three of them a while to coax her up the ladder, but they succeeded and all felt they had scored a big one.

Safely up, Sondra sat square in the middle and smiled, but otherwise was reserved and quiet.

Skip had encouraged Toni to bring her over. "She's not so bad Toni. She just needs some kids to hang around."

Once they were all settled in the treehouse, they began talking about the fair, about Sondra's pageant (to get her to join in the conversation), about the chiffierobe and about Snuff's "beauty show" as Penny put it.

Toni and Sondra told them about their private school and Skip and Penny talked about the big schools they attended and all the things they expected to happen in the coming year. Skip told on himself when he revealed that he'd sworn to his friends at school that he wouldn't let any girls come up in his treehouse, and, now, he had three girls, including his little sister!

Skip and Toni frequently made it a point to draw Sondra out when she seemed to drift away as though they were talking about a culture foreign to her. Slowly Sondra began to relax and enjoy herself and the company of the three kids. Skip even succeeded in getting Sondra to burp and pronounced her a "real kid".

Penny played hostess to them all, pestering and fussing over them with her childish charm.

"It's hard to believe summer is half over already, isn't it? Seems like we just got here." lamented Toni.

"You did" complained Skip "hope you can come sooner next summer." "Yeah" Penny added, "soon as school's out, just like we do."

"Depends on Dad" said Toni absently.

"Toni!" blasted Sondra.

Skip and Penny looked at each other, surprised at Sondra's quick, loud comeback, and then were further confused when they saw that the two girls were blushing

"Uh…I mean…uh…don't you think we should be going Toni?" stammered Sondra.

Toni stood up quickly. "Guess so, Mother will be thinking something horrible has happened like you chipped your nails or something." The group laughed and the tension disappeared.

"Wonder what she'd do if she knew Sondra was in a tree?" Skip suggested.

Sondra shooshed Skip. "She'd….croak!" She pronounced proudly, beginning to enjoy her 'regular kid' status. Everyone laughed as they gathered the picnic up.

After the girls left, Skip and Penny were thoughtful as they walked to the house.

"Wonder what that was all about? Sondra really jumped on Toni" Skip muttered. "Toni seemed to get the message though. There's something going on with their father, don't you think?"

Penny nodded, feeling important that Skip was sharing his thoughts with her. "I never saw their father before." she said

"I met him once" Skip said "he's just about never there, that's all. Can't see anything wrong with that. Dad's gone all week too." They walked around the barn. "Oh well, "he perked up "it's Toni and Sondra we want to see anyhow."

Penny smiled up at Skip. "You were right all along Skip. Sondra's different when she's not around her mother. Boy am I glad about that!" she sighed as she rolled her eyes.

CHAPTER XXV

Revelation

Bill Whitlock left after lunch and promised to return later in the day. He was going into Barlow to meet talk to Mr. Osborne and gather information from the courthouse on some of the Donaldson's dealings. He promised to return later after he called his office in Lincoln.

Frank had come with his truck and he and Jim were in the tool shed. Jim was finishing the installation of the knobs and pulls on the chiffierobe before they the loaded it to take it to the fairgrounds. Meanwhile, Leo was mowing grass to help work off some nervous energy and Stan was back briefly to pack his things for the move the fairgrounds too. Leo was still going to have to stay behind at Jim and Shirley's until things got settled. He mourned the possible loss of two weeks of work at the big fair.

"Why can't you stay here Stan? Mommie could drive you to Barlow everyday! "Penny protested tearfully. "Huh Mommie?" Shirley took a deep breath to explain why that wasn't possible.

Stan knelt down beside Penny. "I told you before Penny, I have to stay there. I have to take care of the animals and the clowns and all the rides. I start about seven o'clock in the morning and I don't quit until about one o'clock the next morning. But I'm planning to come to the reunion picnic. Your Momma says I'm like family now. That makes me feel good."

Penny smiled and hugged Stan. "Okay and I'll take good care of Leo for you." Stan laughed.

"I'm sure you will. Don't give away our secret trick for winning Crazy Eights, okay?"

Penny was astonished. "Does he know how to play crazy eights too?"

Stan felt a bit jealous but nodded "Oh yeah, he's good. He's really good, but just between us, I think you're better."

Penny puffed up with the compliment. "I have lots of 'sperience, that's why."

Shirley called Jim to the phone just as the four younger men finished loading the chiffierobe under Carl's supervision. By the time Jim came back out about ten minutes later the men had come up with a dozen different scenarios. Jim was smiling, causing Leo to sit down on the tailgate and wait hopefully with all his might that there was good news.

"That was my friend Andy at the Plating Company "he told them. He wanted us to know that the police and Bill's guys paid a visit to the outfit next to his shop. Seems they got a real eyeful."

Jim jumped up on the truck bed, pulled a rag from his back pocket and began rubbing out fingerprints on the chiffierobe.

The men exchanged glances. "Jim!" nagged his father, "get on with it, boy."

"Okay, Dad, I will, but I have very few details." Jim looked down at Leo. "They paint trucks in that shop Leo. In fact, when the fellas got there some workers were painting another Donaldson truck. The police uncovered quite an array of stencils and company logos. They copy other companies trucks to the last detail."

Stan scratched his head. "So what does that mean?"

Carl and Leo agreed, blending their words. "I don't get it" and "what's the connection?"

"Well, they aren't entirely sure of how it all comes together, but it seems that the Donaldson's work for an outfit out of St. Louis who steal machinery and materials from places after they have signatures for delivery. They sell them somewhere else in the country. Then the insurance money comes in to replace the stuff and the stuff was never paid for fully to begin with, but the phony paperwork says it was. Guess the police found some evidence of that too. They have somebody on the inside, and work a deal. It's a winner for them both."

"That's a lousy scam" Carl blurted "because somebody knew all along!"

Jim nodded "Oh it is, in fact, it proves someone at the school does know something. Maybe even set it up."

Stan and Leo looked at each other in shock.

"Mr. Osborne?" Stan asked.

"Nooo!" Leo answered in unbelief.

Jim sat down on the wall of the truck bed. "I'm hoping not, that's for sure." Carl protested. I've known Daniel Osborne since the day he interviewed for the job some ten years ago. I won't even entertain that thought. "He turned and walked away.

"I'm with Mr. Chapman" stated Stan flatly "it doesn't necessarily point to him. Trouble is, who does it point to?"

Frank Chapman, who was the quieter of the Chapman boys, spoke up. "The truck was painted to match the construction company trucks, right?"

"Yep," Jim confirmed. "Just like the ones that came and went every day. Just like the ones that were there at night too. All the storage trucks and job trailers."

Leo woke up to a revelation. "That's right!" He threw his hands in the air and poked himself in the temple. "I didn't see the truck close 'cept I remember thinking when it backed up to the service platform that it looked like Ron's old Mack, but it was blue. Ron's is red."

"Seems like a lot of fuss to go through, painting the truck I mean, if Mr. Osborne was in on it." Frank said, simply. "Why would they have to camouflage?"

Jim hopped down off the pick up.

The men were headed toward the shade when Carl returned. "Jim, your mom just reminded me of something."

Everyone turned to Carl. "Roy Donaldson was on the school board when they designed the new wing, wrote the budget, and signed the contracts with Premier Construction."

"Betcha that's it Dad. Betcha anything!"

The men all nodded in agreement.

Leo sighed loudly. He looked at Stan. "Think I might beat the odds, Buddy, there is somebody else gonna take this rap!"

CHAPTER XXVI

Dudes

After a quick supper, all of the men left for Barlow. Skip and Penny went to Frank and Betty's with their son, Eric, who was home from boot camp. He was going to take them on the pontoon along with Sondra and Toni. There would be fireworks all over the lakefront to usher in Fair Week. The kids were giddy with excitement, both at being out on the lake with Eric and with being together. Eric entertained them with funny stories and totally charmed his new neighbors. Toni managed to get Eric to talk about Skip and he willingly obliged with a twisted and exaggerated story about Skip's first campout. Skip wasn't sure how he felt about that; it was kind of embarrassing, but he didn't protest too loudly.

Sondra had rarely ventured out on the water for anything recreational. She had gone on a cruise at one time, but didn't spend time on deck. "Too windy" she complained and retreated to the shops below. Tonight, partly out of curiosity and partly out of desire to be with the other kids, she was the first one on the pontoon. "C'mon Penny, let's get the seats up front" she called back. Toni looked at Skip. "Holy tamollie!"

Late in the evening, Eric dropped the kids off just as Jim pulled in the drive. After some good natured uncle-nephew kidding, Eric left and everyone went into the farmhouse. The kids were chattering at their mother and grandmother when the men, Carl, Jim, Stan and Leo came in the kitchen door, headed for the den and filed into Stan's bedroom. Every one of them carried several shopping bags. Wilma, Shirley and both kids turned in amazement and watched the parade.

Slowly the kitchen gang settled in the den on the sofa and looked at the closed bedroom door from which came loud hoots and whistles, rattling paper, loud whispering. Skip and Penny looked at the ladies and waited for an explanation. Both ladies shrugged.

A few long minutes of waiting paid off when the door opened and one by one the men walked out dressed from head to toe in sparkling new western outfits. Gramps was first, all decked out in black. His shirt had white fringe on the sleeves and white pearl buttons. Except for his white hair, everything else was black.

"Wow gramps! You look terrific!" shouted Skip.

"You look younger, Dad", suggested Shirley.

"Really?" he beamed. Gramma jumped up and went to him smiling.

"Really Carl, she's right" she said as she walked around him.

Next came Leo, whose bright red hair and short beard were complimented by an ivory colored shirt with rust buttons and rust and green embroidery. He wore matching rust colored slacks and ivory boots with fancy stitching. The boots made him taller. The audience oohed and aahed as he strutted across the room and took a bow. He grinned from ear to ear.

Then came Stan who had chosen a more conservative outfit of blue dress jeans and a blue and black checkered shirt with black pearl buttons and black piping. He wore a jean jacket and shiny brown boots. Penny noticed his new hat first, and wrinkled her nose at him as he tipped it to her and winked.

Finally, Jim appeared and caused quite a stir, especially with Shirley who was visibly impressed with his full cut tan western suit, chocolate shirt, tan string tie and brown cowboy boots.

Shirley walked over to Jim. "What's going on? For years I've tried to get you to dress up for the opening day and the square dance but you always end up wearing old suit pants and that faded shirt or something. Jim…" she smiled as she stepped back to get another look "no one will know you!"

"They will after I win my blue ribbon!" he responded, eyes dancing. "Gotta look good for that."

Shirley turned to face the others. "You all look so nice. For once it will really be fun to wear our new dresses, won't it Mom?" she smiled as Wilma walked toward the doorway.

Wilma nodded happily "We can really get gussied up now, as a matter of fact, I have just had a change of plans. I'm not going to wear that blue dress, I just sewed." She turned to Carl. "I have a white dress with black eyelet lace that I made several years ago. That's the one I'm going to wear. C'mon handsome, let's go get it."

Carl looked at her puzzled.

"I want to show Shirley how nicely it will compliment your outfit." she explained.

Carl looked at the men, mocking embarrassment. "I was going to suggest that we do that Honey. Just didn't think these clodhoppers would be nice about it."

"Right Dad thanks." Jim called to them as they left. He reached into his jacket pocket and pulled out a small velveteen box. As Shirley watched, astounded, he fastened a tiny pendant depicting a sunset on a fine gold chain, around her neck.

He smiled, "There, now you're as pretty as me."

Stan cleared his throat and looked at Leo. "Seems like we're forgetting something, doesn't it Leo?"

Leo scratched his beard. "Gee, now that you mention it…I did see some more packages in the bedroom."

Skip and Penny sat quietly on the couch watching and enjoying all that was going on. Penny shot a look at Leo when he said there was something else in the bedroom and caught a twinkle in his eyes. He started to grin as he and Stan walked toward the bedroom and then suddenly turned to the two wide eyed kids, and shouted, "Well come on!"

Both kids bolted off the couch and ran past the laughing men. After less than a minute, Penny shrieked for her mother to come help her dress as she passed her on the fly, looking like a big yellow bag with short little legs. They hurried by Jim and headed for the steps as he was putting his new jacket on a hanger.

Skip could only be heard to say "Wow, thanks! Thanks you guys!" He too scurried to his room to try on his clothes. Stan, Leo and Jim changed clothes and cleaned up the huge mess in Stan's bedroom while everyone was gone. Shortly after they sat down in the kitchen, Carl and Wilma burst through the door. Wilma had her dress "captured" Carl said, in a garment bag. When she "let it out" to show everyone she was nearly hidden by all the layers of crinoline.

Hoping that a big wind didn't knock her off the stage at the dance, Jim smiled "That is very pretty Mom, you two are really going to stop the show."

"I know." Wilma announced proudly as she fingered the new pendant Carl had presented her, at home.

"Gramps look!" shouted Penny from the top of the stairway. She clomped down the steps and twirled around. "I got strings too!" She wore a powder blue satin cowgirl suit with white boots and a white hat to match the white fringe on the shirt and skirt hem. She ran over to Stan and Leo. "Thank you! It's 'nificent!"

Skip entered grinning. "Man, why did you guys do this?" He asked as he admired himself in the hall mirror.

Stan blushed. "Well, we always get something new for the big fairs. Then we thought we'd like to get you kids something too. Your Dad and Grampa argued with us 'til we convinced them that they had better quit fightin us and think about themselves. Got them worried about looking like a couple of scruffs while everyone else here will be gorgeous."

Jim nodded meekly.

Carl raised his hand. "Can I say something here?" He asked as he picked up Penny. "When I saw what they were getting for you kids, I was afraid that you would save all your dances for those drifters, in their dude clothes Penny. So I had to take desperate measures."

Penny laughed at her grandfather and leaned over to whisper in his ear. "You are my first favrite, 'cept Daddy, Gramps. Stan's my second favrite, 'cept Daddy and Leo is my nuther favrite, 'cept Daddy."

"Good!" he announced as he kissed her and put her down to twirl some more.

Skip was parading around the room showing off his new outfit. He wore buckskin colored jeans and a cavalry shirt. The outfit was topped off with what appeared to Shirley to be a faux suede jacket with fringe on the sleeves. He also wore a dark brown hat and cowboy boots that made him taller than his mother. Shirley rubbed the jacket sleeve as she stared at Jim, puzzled.

Jim leaned over and said softly "Don't worry, it's not stolen. They split the cost and I guess Stan just called his mother."

"Called his mother?" Shirley accidentally said aloud. Stan turned and laughed at Shirley whose face was bright red.

He shrugged his shoulders and put out his hands. "I never said she needed my money, I just said I send it to my Mother" he clarified. "She puts it in my account for me." He blushed. Thinks I'm saving it to settle down someday and give her grandkids." He looked at Leo. Leo nodded.

Stan took a breath and cleared his throat. "Don't have any plans for a wife or kids, not yet anyway, but I am thinking, especially with how Leo's being put through this, mostly on account of being a drifter, I'm about ready to settle down. And," he said with emphasis, "I'm thinking…" he paused, checking his decision mentally one more time, "I'll probably settle here, 'least somewhere between here and Barlow."

Penny jumped into Stan's arms and Skip gave him an embarrassed hug. "Yippee!" screeched Penny.

"Guess that says it for all of us, Stan." beamed Jim as he walked over and shook his hand. They immediately began talking about the real estate prospects.

Slowly the group broke up and the kids started up to bed when Bill Whitlock arrived.

"It's all over, guys. The sheriff has arrested the Donaldson brothers and they're having some one picked up with the construction outfit."

They all started celebrating again but this time Leo was the loudest.

"Not guilty" he sang as he danced.

Shirley and Wilma made a pot of coffee and the men went to the den to talk and see if the report was on the news.

After about half an hour Bill came out to the kitchen for some more coffee and "company."

Surprised that Bill would choose their company over the "boys", Shirley and Wilma looked into the den. Jim was snoring loudly on the couch and Carl was asleep in the recliner. Leo was stretched out on the hook rug in front of the fireplace and Higby served as his pillow. Stan had wandered into his bedroom and fell asleep face down stretched across his bed.

"Pops was the first to go" he winked at Wilma "then they all started yawning…couldn't even hear the news, they were so noisy. Guess all that crime fighting wore them out."

Shirley and Wilma looked at him and shook their heads. "No Bill, "laughed Shirley, "it was the shopping."

CHAPTER XXVII

Trouble

"When's Daddy going to get back Mommie" asked Penny as she clomped from window to window in her new boots. She was watching for her father to return in the van and also kept her eye out for Skip who had ridden his bike to get Toni.

Mrs. Chapman was concentrating on tying a small blue gingham bow on Snuff's collar.

"He said he'd be back by nine. You're not excited are you?" she teased.

"I just can't wait Mommie! This is the most exciting day of the whole year."

Mrs. Chapman reflected on that statement. "Oh I don't know. Seems to me we have had a great deal of excitement this year. Let's hope if there are any more surprises that they are good ones."

"Yah" agreed Penny "like Daddy winning a blue ribbon."

Mrs. Chapman looked at her daughter curiously "Well how about Snuff and Sondra?"

Penny looked at Snuff laying in the middle of the kitchen floor in a sunbeam. "Oh them too but I want Daddy to win the most. He 'zerves it."

"He sure does Penny" smiled her mother in approval.

Penny glanced out the window. "Here come Skip and Toni!" she shouted as she ran out the door.

Shirley picked up the sleepy cat and placed her in her travel cage. "There you go Pretty Girl, better go back to sleep. You have a big day ahead of you."

A car door slammed and Shirley looked up to see Jim's parents approaching the kids in the yard. "Everything's ready here on the table Dad," she called.

Today was the big Chapman family reunion and Gramma and Grampa were going to take all the coolers and baskets of food to the pavilion while Jim and Shirley went to the pet show with Penny.

Shortly after that car was loaded, Jim pulled in and following some last minute planning they all piled into the vehicles and headed for the fairgrounds.

Penny could barely contain herself in her excitement and chattered faster than ever all the way to the fairgrounds, but when her foot hit the ground in the parking lot, she stopped talking and she spent every ounce of energy on taking in all the sights and sounds and smells of opening day.

After checking out the competition at the arts tent and making sure the chiffierobe was all buffed up, Penny and her parents headed for the pet show that was to begin in less than an hour.

Skip and Toni were helping his grandparents unload the car and then they were planning to go over to the pet show.

Penny cooed to Snuff and promised her a nice treat after the pet show. "Daddy's going to buy you a 'nilla cone Snuff, just for being in the pet show! You don't even have to win. Isn't that nice?" Penny smiled at her dad. "Snuff says thank you."

"Oh she did, huh, did she say we should get one for you too?" he asked. Penny thought. "I think so."

Jim laughed, and then stopped suddenly, signaling Penny to hush. "Did you hear someone call my name Shirley?" He asked, listening carefully.

"Jim Chapman! Where are you?" cried a voice that sounded a lot like Skip, but not exactly. The threesome turned around to see Skip and Toni searching frantically down both aisles of the long barn.

"Here Son!" Jim yelled as he moved up the aisle amidst the loud barking of several caged dogs.

Skip spotted him. "Dad! Get Mom! Hurry! Skip and Toni raised dust as they spun around and led Jim, Shirley and Penny out of the barn and around to the side to a shortcut to the picnic grove.

"He collapsed Dad" Skip cried loudly. "He insisted on helping us set up chairs. Uncle Frank is…"he gasped for air, "trying to revive him!"

Just then a loud siren blew scaring everyone and causing gooseflesh to rise on Jim and Shirley's arms and necks. Penny screamed and her dad turned back and scooped her up. When they arrived, breathless, at the pavilion a Barlow paramedic unit was working on Uncle Pete.

Penny buried her face in her dad's shoulder to keep from screaming when she caught a glimpse of the old man's ashen face and limp body.

Gramma and Aunt Sally were crying and Inez was climbing into the ambulance while the paramedics were loading Pete into the back.

Frank walked over to his Mother quickly and hugged her and then climbed into the ambulance without saying anything.

Gramps was giving another paramedic some information about what Pete was doing when he collapsed. Shirley worked her way over to be with Wilma who was very concerned by now, with Aunt Sally.

Jim and several others settled the younger children and ushered them out of the way of the ambulance that was pulling away with the siren blaring.

The shocked family gathered back together and talked. Every few minutes someone else arrived for the reunion and they were told about the incident. Everyone spoke in hushed tones.

After about an hour, Jim and Shirley returned. They had taken Sally to the hospital to be checked and to be with Pete, if that was possible.

"We were able to talk to Dr. Braemer after he checked Aunt Sally. She's going to be okay, but she needs to stay in the hospital overnight."

People nodded, but no one spoke. "Dr. Braemer "he continued "said Unce Pete suffered a stroke. He said he's stable now and he has high hopes that not much damage was done. They're going to do a lot of tests, but he said it looks good."

The solemn crowd broke into cheers. Folks started moving around and began settling in for the reunion. Jim and Shirley greeted family members as they worked their way toward the back of the pavilion, where the kids were.

Jim had told Shirley they needed to find Penny. Shirley lowered her head. "Poor little thing."

Jim searched the group and moved out of the shelter when he didn't locate her. Finally, he found Penny sitting with some children on the jungle gym in the middle of the park. Several older kids tossed a ball nearby. "Penny" he said soberly, "I'm afraid you missed the pet show and Snuff would be disqualified without a handler."

Penny looked up at her father, unable to hide her disappointment.

"I forgot all about it Daddy, 'til too late" she said sadly, her eyes drifting toward the direction of the barns. Then she brightened "But Skip said Uncle Pete and Aunt Sally are going to get better!" she smiled bravely. Then she stood up as though she were eighty years old herself. "I better go tell Snuff though" she said seriously.

Skip and Toni walked over. "We'll take her, Dad."

CHAPTER XXVIII

Disqualified

Toni held Penny's hand as they walked out of the grove. Penny was feeling very mixed up. Toni understood and talked softly about other things, cheering Penny and Skip both up, considerably. Before they were even to the opening of the barn the trio heard a familiar voice.

"So… here you are!"

All three stopped suddenly when they saw Toni's mother just inside the doorway. She was furious.

"What are you doing in this…" she threw her arms up…"barn?"

The kids looked at one another, confused. The barn was quiet. Very few people were in sight anywhere around it and the few animals that remained in cages were sleeping or too tired to care. The kids moved up closer to the door and spotted Sondra standing alone down at the far end of aisle one. She had a frightened look on her face.

Toni signaled for Penny to be quiet when Penny turned to ask her a question.

Mrs. Burroughs stomped up to Sondra and grabbed her arm.

"Why in the world are you in here? Do you know what you have done? You, young lady, have been disqualified! "She screeched.

She threw Sondra's arm down, hard. "What do you have to say for yourself?" She leaned into Sondra's face "And it had better be good!"

Sondra flushed and stepped back. "P…P..Penny's uncle had a heart attack or something" she croaked. I heard about an emergency in the grove and saw Skip and Toni run over here" she faltered, unable to breathe comfortably "but I got mixed up in the people and didn't know where they went. I just wanted to ask what happened. Some lady told me." She looked wide-eyed at her mother who had stiffened her back and folded her arms. Sondra wrung her hands. "I was going to go back over to my place for the interviews, but I remembered the rules about the pets have to have a handler. The judges were coming in so I just…"

"Stayed here for a stupid cat? "her mother asked in amazement. Sondra's eyes filled with tears, but her face took on a different expression.

"No! I didn't stay for the cat!" She took a deep breath.

Mrs. Burroughs threw up her hands again and poked out her chin. "Oh really?"

Sondra's voice was cracking. She squeezed out the words. "I stayed here for Penny! She's my friend Mother. She's a nice girl …and I like her!" She stabbed at her tears. "She and Skip are my only friends!"

Penny put her fingers in her mouth and felt tears trickle down her face and quivering chin.

Sondra's mother turned to the wall. She noticed the three others but ignored them as she turned back, armed for another assault. Her expression alarmed Skip.

"Sondra, we have spent three whole weeks and a lot of money, mind you, getting you ready for this pageant. I can't believe you threw your chances away. It was all so important to you!"

Sondra looked up at her mother and shook her head furiously. "Important to me?" she cried "Oh no…" she succumbed to her tears.

Skip felt a pain in his throat as he caught Toni brushing angrily at her tears, out of the corner of his eye. Penny was sniffling, fighting to keep quiet.

"*You* want me to be a beauty queen Mother. *You* want me to be a perfect little lady" she sobbed. "And that was okay 'til now. When I watch Skip and Toni having so much fun and Penny's always asking me to come and play and I can't…" She swallowed and took a deep breath. "I can't even get dirty, Mother. It's not fair!" Sondra covered her face with her hands. "I want to be like them! I just want to be a regular kid!" she cried, muffling her words with her hands.

Skip smiled as he held his emotions in check.

Toni started to go to Sondra, but stopped when Sondra took another loud, deep breath and stepped closer to her mother.

"Maybe Mother, if you weren't so busy with me and if you didn't expect Daddy to work so hard all the time…" she paused, aware of her mother's changing expression, "maybe he would come home more… instead of staying in town drinking all night. Maybe we could be a family againnn." Sondra choked on her words and slumped down onto the dusty barn floor in her new designer dress.

When Sondra sat down, Snuff's cage was visible, as was a big red ribbon and a certificate, stapled to the table.

Mrs. Burroughs stood very still, her shock at Sondra's rebellion all over her face.

Toni hurried over to Sondra, helped her up and gave her a long hug, as they cried. Then, smiling through her tears she said "I'm so proud of you Sunny." Sunny smiled at her, but sadly. Toni turned to her stunned mother. "You should be too."

CHAPTER XXIV

The Real Reunion

Toward evening, the Chapmans were all together again at the pavilion. Mrs. Burroughs had left, with Toni and Sondra. Before leaving, she stared, in disbelief, at the cage and then at Skip and Penny. Penny edged to Skip's backside.

When the Burroughs left the siblings walked back to the pavilion, heartsick. They hung around the relatives, but didn't have much luck shaking off the scene they had witnessed in the barn. Skip situated Snuff's cage on a empty table the kids talked to family that stopped to admire the ribbon and certificate.

Jim and Shirley brought the kids ice cream that Eric and Frank had just made and were scooping a bite into Snuff's dish when Skip jumped up.

"Toni, you came back!" The Chapmans all turned to greet Toni and were surprised to see Sondra and Mrs. Burroughs behind her.

Mrs. Burroughs walked directly over to Penny and Skip. Penny slowly reached for her dad's hand, intimidated by the stately woman.

"I really don't know how to say this," Mrs. Burroughs began, "but I am so sorry you had to be involved in our problems."

Skip stammered "Well uh...we..."

She raised her hand and Skip flinched in spite of himself.

"I am trying to say thank you. Thank you for being so good to my girls." She bit her lip as she patted his face.

"Our girls!" corrected a husky voice.

Toni jumped as though electricity had gone through her.

Mrs. Burroughs turned into the arms of her husband and the sisters shouted. "Daddy!"

"Chuck Burroughs" he said as he offered his hand to Jim, then Shirley and finally, Skip. "Skip!" he bellowed.

"Hi Mr. Burroughs...Um, nice to see you again," Skip managed to say, in his shock.

Mr. Burroughs laughed. "Momma here called me. Said we had better get our act together. Said our kids are acting more like the grown ups and we are..." he looked at Toni and Sondra.. "and said we are going to miss out on the best part of our lives the way we're going. Time to get with it!"

Toni and Sondra grabbed their parents. "Are you going to stay here?" Toni asked, hopefully.

"Sure are, gonna square dance." Chuck said, humored.

"You are?" Sondra asked flabbergasted.

"Sure, we always used to!"

Toni was bug-eyed. "You did?"

"Yeees'um. Now how about introducing us to your friends?"

Toni and Sondra took their parents hands and proudly marched them around the pavilion, introducing them to everyone.

The last light of day filtered through the beams of the old pavilion. Skip took Penny's shoulders and squeezed them as they watched their parents talk and laugh with the Burroughs. Penny squealed with delight when Jim tied his blue ribbon to his lapel. And if that wasn't enough, she jumped and twirled her "strings" when he acknowledged Mrs. Burroughs congratulations, and she told him, "Just call me Pat."

The End

www.ingramcontent.com/pod-product-compliance
Lightning Source LLC
LaVergne TN
LVHW041611070526
838199LV00052B/3088